Cold Wide Open Eyes

A Hugo Storm Crime Thriller, Volume 2

Anton Lindbak

Published by Cold Bird Books, 2019.

COLD WIDE OPEN EYES

A Hugo Storm Crime Thriller

by

ANTON LINDBAK

Copyright 20©19: 20©20 – Anton Lindbak

ALL RIGHTS RESERVED

FIRST EDITION – MARCH 2019

THIS BOOK IS A WORK OF FICTION

Any resemblance to real people, living or dead, private entities or events are entirely coincidental.

Thank you to my Editor - D.K.T

Further thanks to the great team of Cold Bird Books for cover design and publishing support.

This book is dedicated to my good friend Toby Kunkel - a great man - cheers brother!

ONE

"I want my money back!"

Father Angus Black looked hard at the tumbler of single malt on the table in front of him. Hadn't I heard that before? But at least, this time, I wasn't the one on the hook. I didn't reply; I waited. The Father had called my office earlier this morning, requesting a meeting – urgently. I had hesitated at first, but then he promised it would be worth it. I knew the man, and I didn't like him. But as always, I needed money – so I accepted his request. We agreed to meet at The Tap, Charlie Thomson's bar just off George Street, down-town Edinburgh, at ten that morning. The Tap was a fine establishment, open from early to late, where many discreet conversations could be held in confidence.

"You know Julia Felt, don't you?"

The good Father continued before licking his lips and draining off the fine whisky. A big guy in his late forties, possibly handsome to some – in a brutish sort of way. His obvious thirst for the demon drink was starting to leave its mark, but, undoubtedly, the man had a presence with his bald, shiny head, piercing, deep-set brown eyes and neatly trimmed goatee. His suit was black and tailored. Not your average clergyman: yes, he wore the collar of a priest and carried a Bible, but I knew he was nothing but a gangster, and a dangerous one too. His dark eyes radiated the unmistakeable look of a man totally comfortable with violence.

"Yeah, I know Julia Felt – she owes you money?" I asked, surprised, taking a sip of my coffee. It was getting tepid. Angus gave a tight grin; I knew the man had a temper.

"Yes, she does Hugo, and you're going to find her for me."

His using my first name and stating what sounded like a command annoyed me, but before I could answer, the good Father stood up abruptly and pointed to his empty whisky glass.

"I need another, you want one Hugo?"

I shook my head, I didn't drink much alcohol, never liked the fuzzy sensation it brought to my head.

"No thanks Angus, I'm fine."

I smiled and leaned back, whilst holding his gaze. He looked at me as if I'd cursed his God, before heading over to the bar, where Charlie Thomson was busily employed. Charlie, all dapper and neat as usual, often worked the bar by himself. The place was popular with the shadier characters of Edinburgh's business community, and many scams and hustles were agreed in hushed conversations by the bar, where Charlie himself often conducted a few dubious deals in winks, looks and cryptic talk. I loved the place.

The Father returned with another crystal tumbler of Charlie's finest and, without doubt, most expensive single malt. Neither Charlie nor anybody else had so much as raised an eyebrow at a Catholic priest downing whisky so early in the morning. But then again, this was The Tap; whatever was said and done in The Tap stayed in The Tap.

I observed Father Angus as he approached the table, the tumbler almost comically small in his beefy hand. I was reasonably well acquainted with Julia Felt and I liked her, although I hadn't really seen her much in the last few years. She was a professional poker player who had clawed her way out of a miserable, chaotic childhood by means of sheer determination. I remembered her telling me, over a drink years ago, that she had decided in her early teenage years not to be defined by her drug-addict mother and unknown father. The intensity with which she told me this had stuck in my mind. So, I knew this lady was not only beautiful, but strong, determined and capable. How she had become involved with Father Black intrigued me. I wasn't going to facilitate Julia's being hurt by this gangster priest. But I was curious and wanted to know what was going on. Also, if I didn't find her, Angus would get somebody else, and I doubted they would be as sympathetic towards Julia as I was.

"So, Angus, what's going on?" I asked, glancing at my wristwatch. It was an expensive Swiss make, solid and dependable, and so it should be considering the price of the thing. I had another meeting coming up, and time was getting tight, so I needed this to move on. Angus didn't answer, just looked at me with a smirk forming on his lips. The atmosphere between us changed; I felt the vibe turn sour. It wasn't as if the man could be characterised as jovial at the best of times, but the look he now gave me was sinister.

"Right, Angus, what do you want from me?" I asked again, in an aggressive tone of voice, holding his eyes. Bring it on, I thought as I watched Father Angus lean forward, his smirk still plainly visible.

"You know about the poker game on Saturday?"

"You're talking about Cameron Bullard's game?" I replied coldly.

"Yeah, that's the one. I fronted the entry money for Julia."

Angus paused, studying me as I digested what he had said. It was another surprise. Julia playing in a game – an illegal game – hosted by Edinburgh's most senior gangster was not something I'd expected. She wasn't an angel by any means, but taking part in a high-stake illegal poker game hosted by a dangerous gangster wasn't something I would've put her down for. The risks involved seemed to me to be above her tolerance range. There were plenty of wealthy potential clients with a taste for gambling, but a lack of ability, who approached her to 'invest', and plenty of legit games worldwide where she would be welcomed with open arms. Her clients would front the necessary money and sign a legally-binding agreement to share the winnings as well as any potential losses. I had heard that Julia, on average, won 8 out of 10 games she played.

"Right." I simply acknowledged his statement and waited.

"We're talking a lot of money here, Hugo. A chair at the table was a cool 500K, but the pot was equally as big. Cameron went all out this year. Julia assured me she would win ... you get that? Guaranteed!"

He stopped, looked at the whisky, licked his lips again, then gave in and drained the glass. I doubted Julia would've said that, it didn't sound like her at all – too unprofessional. But there was definitely something going on here. I tapped the table lightly.

"She approached you to front the money?" I asked, determined to dig deeper. If I was going to accept this, then I wanted to know as much detail as possible. Many of my clients withheld information from me, having agendas they wouldn't divulge. I didn't take that personally, it came with the territory. Being lied to was part of the job.

"No, not directly, we were linked up by somebody we both know." Again, he paused, keeping his eyes on me. The smirk evolved into a full grin; I felt a small burn of anger deep down, but quenched it before it surfaced. The man had wanted me to ask, so I had. This was not going quite the way I'd anticipated.

"Who?"

"You!" rasped Angus hoarsely, flashing a solid set of nicotine-stained teeth.

Silence fell as I digested what he'd just said. The atmosphere dropped from cold to sub-zero. I rolled my shoulders in an effort to control my temper. The temptation to lash out was almost overwhelming – almost. I leaned forward, my hands flat on the table. He was bigger in bulk, but I could still take him out. Angus knew this too; he tensed up, the smirk gone, waiting for my move.

"Say again, Angus?" I managed to maintain a controlled, calm tone. Lose control of yourself, and you have already lost the play! That had been the advice given to my brother and me by our father, Frank Storm, the legendary Norwegian hard man and fixer. Advice I had tried to adhere to – well, most of the time. My brother: not as much.

"You heard! You, Hugo, the big-time fixer and all, getting desperate, running short of money, wanting to make the big score. Whatever ... point is, Cameron would believe it."

I shook my head. My muscles screaming to unleash on the vicious man sitting in front of me. "Rubbish! He wouldn't – why should I do something like that?" I protested, fighting the sense of being on the defensive.

"You really want to find out if Cameron wouldn't believe it?" Angus paused for a moment, sensing he had the upper hand. "Didn't he take your house five months ago? To cover that debt? Didn't that make your second wife take the kids and leave you? Helena, yeah, Helena. I remember seeing her a few years ago, what a stunner, man! You must be so flamin' angry, Hugo. Yeah, not greed – revenge is better. Cameron will buy that."

Angus paused again, his tone one of triumph. He studied me as I reeled in shock. I hadn't seen that coming. I forced myself to sit still and let him talk. My time would come. Angus was on a roll; I didn't want to stop him just yet. He leaned forward, his eyes now pulsing with hatred.

"Hugo, underneath the surface you're just like the rest of us mortals. For your benefit I'll say it again: revenge and for good measure maybe desperation. I mean those lawyer's fees are stacking up, aren't they? Anyway, who cares! You doubt Cameron will buy this? Trust me, I can sell it to him if I need to."

I knew he could, I also knew he was desperate himself, and desperate men do desperate things. This guy would stab his own mother for a dime, no doubt! He also had an insurance: I was convinced that he was capable of that. The guy was street smart, if I took him out, word would somehow get to Cameron Bullard. Even from beyond the grave, Angus would get to me.

Tapping the table lightly with my fingers, I allowed myself to breathe, steadying the ship, controlling my emotions. I could fix this, I could fix anything, but I needed time to get a grip on it all. "Why me?" I asked.

"Because Julia trusts you! You're the best – and I want my blasted money! I know you'll agree, Hugo, there's nothing like an incentive to get a job done well, is there?" Angus chuckled hoarsely as he said this, no doubt feeling very pleased with himself.

"Right." I gave in; the man had me where he wanted me – for now. And he'd been clever enough to get me to come to this meeting with my guard down.

"When was the last time you heard from her?" I moved the dialogue on.

"Saturday night, but not a peep since then. I went looking yesterday, but nothing; nobody knows where she is. Her usual numbers are unavailable. It's as if she's dropped into a black hole and disappeared."

The previous smug amusement in Angus' face had now gone, replaced by a small twitch in his right eye. I looked at him again and realised he was nervous. The man was now messing about with Cameron Bullard, and had nothing to show for it either. I knew greed had made him pursue this, it was the only fuel for men like him, and now he was thinking he'd been cheated by Julia. Such is life if you're a bottom feeder. He knew that messing with Cameron Bullard was incredibly dangerous – terminal in fact if Cameron got wind of it. It wouldn't just be me that would be heading for the Firth of Forth, wearing concrete boots if this reached Cameron – Angus would be following swiftly. But most importantly, I had to make sure I wasn't taken out first.

"I'll find her and get your money back, but you've got to give me some time here. It won't be easy to track her down."

"I'll give you seventy-two hours, Hugo. After that, who knows?"

"I'll take half of what I recover for you, Angus, and I'll let you walk away from this in one piece. You got that?"

Angus laughed, a harsh cold laugh that descended into a coughing fit. I sat and waited; maybe he would manage to suffocate himself?

His face turned deep red, but he managed to recover his composure. Shame! Then he leaned forward, aggressive once more; he wasn't finished yet.

"You Storm boys think you're something special, don't you? Above us nasties, with your private schooling and your fancy Norwegian heritage. But remember, you've done time too – how long was it? Eighteen months in Edinburgh Central? Listen, Hugo – Cameron Bullard might've owed a debt to your father back in the day, but do you think that'll protect you forever?"

I didn't, and the angry priest had yet again served me a curveball that I hadn't seen coming. Cameron Bullard owed my father? News to me. I knew dad had frequently been in Scotland on business before he was killed, but I hadn't been aware of any relationship between him and Cameron. Neither my father nor Cameron had ever mentioned that. It was something to investigate, but not now. I had a plateful here to deal with first.

"Calm down, Angus! I'll fix this, but I always get paid."

I tried to stay calm, whilst holding his stare. It took some effort, but I'd been face-to-face with many a predator before; back down in these situations, and you're nothing but prey. Angus shook his head.

"Consider your continued existence as payment enough."

I didn't reply. It was obvious that he wasn't going to pay me; under no circumstances would he do so.

"I hear you." I stood up.

"That-a-boy! Call me on the mobile number on the card when you've found her." Angus dropped a business card on the table.

I ignored his patronising words, picked up the card and dropped it in the pocket of my black leather jacket. Angus didn't look up, instead he brought out his mobile phone, opened the clock app and chose the timer function. Then he pressed start. We both looked at the screen as the seconds started to run.

"Seventy-two hours, Hugo. You better get going!" Angus didn't bother to look up.

I took a deep breath – yet again stopping myself from lashing out. This was just Angus playing the dominance game, cheap and pathetic in some ways, but also very real. The consequences of Angus' proposal could be devastating; if you messed with Cameron on something he valued dearly, he would retaliate tenfold. I knew for a fact that he highly valued this poker game. I also had no doubt whatsoever Angus would convince him of my involvement. Whatever debt Cameron owed to our father, I doubted that it would prevent his giving the order to kill me. At the end of the day, Frank Storm was long gone. I was about to move, when Angus looked up.

"And if you think you can screw me on this, Hugo, then think again pal!" He pointed to his eyes. "Remember, Cold, Wide-Open Eyes."

TWO

"You are totally screwed!"

As I entered my office, Jimmy Johnson spat out these words at me without even looking up from his laptop. Glancing back at him, I tried to break a smile, but with my mood in a lousy state it didn't work.

"What about my brother?" I asked as I walked towards my grand, funky, metal desk.

"He's screwed too!" Jimmy laughed, still not looking up from his laptop.

Sometimes I wondered how I managed to like this guy, and just now I wasn't in the mood for banter. But Jimmy didn't know that, so I let it slide.

Jimmy Johnson, who represented both my brother and me, was a hard-charging lawyer and a ruthless street-fighter: the type of guy you wanted on your side when the wolves came from all directions. He was a working-class kid from the rough side of Glasgow, who despite growing up in poverty, had fought himself through law school and had gone on to become a barrister. The guy possessed heaps more determination, intelligence and savvy than the slick, privileged kids who graduated from the very best law schools. Carrying a chip on his shoulder about the size of Glasgow, he radiated the energy of someone with a lot to prove. But he did so for the most part, in my view, with class. Not that everybody saw it that way. Jimmy enjoyed metaphorically 'flipping the bird' to the establishment – one of the main reasons I couldn't help but like the man.

He was sitting on my comfortable sofa with his laptop up and running, presumptuously connected to my Wi-Fi and no doubt billing someone else as we spoke. Jimmy didn't lose a minute billing a client – and why should he? Nobody had handed Jimmy the life he now had; he'd studied, worked and hustled like mad for every penny he had. That was another reason why I liked the guy: Jimmy was good at what he did and made no excuses for being ruthless doing it.

I shook myself out of my black leather jacket, draped it across the back of my office chair and went over to my stylish lounge area. My office was smart, kitted out in a funky Scandinavian design. The expensive kind, not IKEA. I liked nice design, particularly Scandinavian, but then again I was Norwegian by birth. My office was purposely expensive-looking; the trappings of success attract business, like honey attracts bees. Now, since I'd lost my home, my office was multi-tasking, but I kept any evidence of this out of sight. Initially this had been a flat, but I'd converted it to an office years ago whilst retaining a private bathroom as well as office facilities. The file room now doubled as a bedroom – not exactly cosy, but comfortable enough.

Clearing his throat and replacing his smile with his serious face, Jimmy continued, "But you know, Hugo, you don't need to be screwed."

I sat down on a chair opposite him and let out a sigh. I knew where this was going. "Right Jimmy – how?"

"Let me take off the gloves and get this sorted."

"No." I shook my head. "No way, Jimmy!" My words carried the force of my conviction.

"Hugo, what do you want? I'm fighting this case – your case – with both my hands tied behind my back. Do you want to win?"

Jimmy had placed his laptop on the sofa and was leaning forward, locking my gaze with a pair of cold, analytical eyes. Jimmy loved banter, but when it was time for business there was no joking.

"It's not about winning," I protested, staring back intensely. "This is not a war."

My words sounded pathetic, even to my own ears, and Jimmy rolled his eyes in response, taking a moment before he spoke again.

"Listen, Hugo, you're smart and clever. You're also a decent guy, but you're not doing yourself any favours here by playing the knight in shining armour. Of course, it's war!"

I felt my temper ignite, not because he was wrong but because he was right, but still I couldn't give him what he wanted – and probably what I needed.

"Jimmy, we're talking about Claire and Emily here. I obviously love Emily, but I still care about Claire too!" My words sounded defensive, but I knew how I felt. I still believed – maybe that should be hoped – that Claire would come around. Sure, she would see reason, or so I prayed.

"I know we're talking about Claire and Emily. I know them both, unless you've forgotten. I'm Emily's Godfather for goodness sake. Remember back in the day when you, Claire, me and whichever girl I was dating at the time, used to go out dancing and having fun together? Good old days. But that was then and this is now."

I nodded as I forced my temper to fizzle out.

"I know," I said and paused before continuing, "I just want access to Emily – just like it used to be. But I'm not willing to create mayhem to get that back. It would just cause bitterness and resentment. It'd hurt Claire, and that would hurt Emily. If I caused her mother any harm, how could I look Emily in the eyes again? No, that's not me. That will not happen. So, you play this one nice, Jimmy – and that's final."

Jimmy was about to say something but realising the futility of trying to sway my mind, he held back. Instead, he looked at me for a moment, then smiled again. "Okay. You got it. You're the boss, Hugo. Still …"

"I know – I'm totally screwed!"

Jimmy laughed, breaking the tension. He was a good-looking guy, if you didn't focus too much on his nose. It'd been badly broken in his late teens in a boxing match, putting a stop to his fledging career, but Jimmy wore it as a badge of honour. Coming from the rough part of Glasgow, it was part of his tough-guy image, but with Jimmy there was actually substance behind that image. He liked the bad-boy persona, it sat just right and tight with him. The toffs in his profession, with their wigs, stilted speech and privileged backgrounds were terrified of Jimmy. And rightly so; he ran rings around most them in the courtroom.

"So, what's your next move for Douglas?"

I had decided to shelve the dramatic new development of that morning until after this meeting with Jimmy. I hadn't even entertained the thought of informing him about this just yet. Maybe later, depending on what route I decided to pursue. Jimmy was a friend, but even with friends there are things one prefers to keep to oneself. Jimmy was also a lawyer, and hence his hands would be tied in a legal, professional sense if I dropped him into this before I'd got the lay of the land. The whole thing might just spiral even further out of control. I decided to keep Jimmy out of this for now.

"We're going to court on Wednesday. Less than seventy-two hours, Hugo boy. It's about to start." Jimmy paused and looked at me hard. "The gloves are off on that one; yes?"

"Yes, definitely. Do whatever you can get away with," I said, and meant it.

Regardless of the latest development, this was separate business and Jimmy could do whatever he did best, being the brutally-efficient lawyer he was. My brother had taken the fall alone when my life had fallen apart six months ago, just as he'd promised to do. Not once, as far as I was aware, had he implicated me, even when they'd pushed on about me. I had friends in Police Scotland, but I had enemies there too, and at this present time the latter were in the majority. Douglas' former employer, Police Scotland, was coming for him with a vengeance.

Couldn't blame them really; Douglas had broken just about every law there was and had dragged their reputation through the mud. I would've been fuming with him too. Some of that hostility was rubbing off on me. It was fair to say, the Storm boys in general were not popular within the Scottish police community.

"Cool ..." Jimmy paused and glanced at me with thoughtful eyes.

"What, Jimmy?"

"You talked to Douglas lately?"

I shook my head. Jimmy was a smart guy and was as well-connected as me, knowing as many shady characters in Scotland's criminal underworld as I did. I wondered if he'd heard any whispers about Julia, Father Black, and this poker game. A part of me wanted to share, but I needed to hear what he had say first. I didn't play cards or gamble any more but I still preferred to keep my cards close to my chest, especially when my gut instinct told me to wait.

"Well, not for the last couple of weeks. What's up?"

I felt my heart rate rise up a notch. A week or two in the life of Douglas Storm was a long time. As had been proven, mayhem could erupt at any time.

"Probably nothing, just that the guard I've got looking out for Douglas tells me he seems to be a little ... let's say, a little shifty." Jimmy paused, his intense eyes scanning me before he continued, "He's probably nervous about the trial. Can you blame him?"

We looked at each other for what seemed like an age. I knew Jimmy was holding something back, and for a brief, intense moment I debated with myself in silence as to whether or not I should probe. Something told me not to, the vibe I was picking up from Jimmy just didn't sit right.

"Yeah, I guess so," I replied, ending the silence.

Jimmy took a sip from the glass of iced-water on the coffee table, then gestured towards me with his right hand. "Anyway, I'll keep you informed, Hugo ... You coming to court on Wednesday?"

I grimaced, it wasn't something I wanted to do. Nonetheless, I knew I ought to.

"Well, Jimmy – yes. I had planned to anyway."

"Good, Douglas will appreciate that. He's the first case of the day. You better be early, its going to be a circus."

Jimmy laughed as he turned to pick up and put away his laptop into its leather bag. I looked at the man, thinking I was maybe just being paranoid here. What could Jimmy possibly be holding back? Still, I decided to withhold the events of this morning until I'd digested them myself.

"Listen, Hugo, I've gotta go – gotta take mum to her doctor's appointment. Another cancer scare coming up." Jimmy broke a sad grin as he got up.

"Yeah sure, Jimmy," I said as I got up too, sensing the atmosphere between us had become somewhat tense. "How's Mary anyway?" My question, though a bit lame, was genuine. I knew Jimmy's mother well; she was a tough Glaswegian with a heart of gold, who'd brought up her four kids single-handedly.

"Oh, you know her, a proper battle-axe. She'll face down this cancer as she had the others. The woman is simply indestructible."

"She certainly is, she'll outlive us all," I remarked, as we shook hands.

"No doubt, Hugo, no doubt. Anyway, I'll keep you posted. Do me a favour: carefully consider exactly what you want to do about Emily's custody case."

"Will do, Jimmy," I replied.

"Good man."

Jimmy punched my shoulder lightly as he turned to leave. I followed as far as my office door, then watched him stride past Petite's desk, heading for the exit.

THREE

I looked on as Petite Williams, my very capable assistant, exchanged a look with Jimmy as he walked past her desk. Was that a look of passion? I couldn't tell, but a few years ago, the morning after a New Year's party at my house, I'd been shocked to find Petite and Jimmy in a compromising position. Blurting out an embarrassed apology, I'd beaten a hasty retreat from the room. Immediately afterwards, it had seemed quite funny, but it wasn't funny now; something wasn't right about Jimmy; the most frustrating part was that I couldn't put my finger on it. I fixed my eyes on his back as he walked through the door, but he didn't look round. What on earth had just happened? Without realising it, I was clenching my fists. A cough from Petite got my attention and I glanced over. Her head tilted slightly to one side, curiosity written all over her face.

"You okay Hugo?"

"If you've got a minute Petite, we need to talk," I answered flatly, gesturing for her to come to my office.

"Sure," said Petite, getting up from her chair.

I walked back into my office and was putting the kettle on as she entered. I kept my back to her as my brain went into overdrive. I trusted Petite, without any caveats, always had. A look between her and Jimmy shouldn't – couldn't – change that. I pulled myself together; was I letting paranoia take hold of me?

"You fancy a cuppa?"

"Yes please. Green tea, if you don't mind," chirped Petite as she sat down on the sofa.

"Coming up," I said, trying to clear my head. I would continue to trust Petite, and come back to Jimmy at another time.

I fixed her a green tea and a strong black coffee for myself.

"So, how did the meeting go, Hugo?" Petite asked as she took her cup from me.

I sat down opposite her, sipped my coffee and cleared my throat. Leaning back, I took a breath, "Badly," I replied.

"Really, how?"

"I'm being blackmailed." There was silence. I wasn't sure how much she wanted to know about this, but Petite didn't reply, so I continued, glancing at her as I asked, "You know about the poker game on Saturday, Cameron's game, don't you?"

Petite straightened herself up, tilting her head as she did when intrigued. "Yes, who doesn't? What about it?"

"The game was rigged, by Julia Felt. She got Father Angus Black to front the money on the promise of a sure fix."

"Wow, that's crazy!" Petite replied, stunned. She shook her head, continuing, "Doesn't make any sense, I mean who in their right mind would mess with Cameron Bullard's game. It's his precious baby. Vanity project, or whatever you want to call it."

"Well, yes, I agree but that's not all," I replied.

"Unless Cameron rigged the game himself – I could buy that, but it's pretty thin – and why would he do it?" Petite's mind was racing.

I shook my head emphatically. "No, he wouldn't, and he didn't, but Julia did."

Petite looked at me intensely. Her purple hair, the colour of the month, was styled in a hip sort of way. Her pursed blood-red lips were bursting with questions. "Why would Julia do that?"

I lifted my arms in a frustrated gesture and said, "Beats me, but Angus says she did, and now she's gone underground. Whatever happened, I don't think it went to plan, and now Angus is livid. He wants his money back!"

"Right, so where's the blackmail? What's your part in this mess?"

"I've got to find Julia for Angus, and fast – he gave me seventy-two hours – or he'll shop me in to Cameron, tell him I was behind the rigging of the game."

Petite's brain was working on full steam. She had the knack of seeing things that I, at times, overlooked. "If Angus does that, he'll be signing his own death warrant. He knows that, so he's planned a way to drop the whole mess on you and Julia." Petite grimaced before continuing, "It's probably a rubbish plan, but nonetheless ..."

"Yes, that's what I figured myself. I'm pretty sure Angus' plan won't hold either, but that's not the point. I'd rather not be his concrete-booted, fish-food buddy at the bottom at the Forth!"

"Mm, yeah, but you know, Hugo, even if you find Julia this won't be over."

"Nope, it won't, I know that Petite," I growled. Petite's eyes narrowed, and I lifted my hands by way of apology, "Sorry Petite, just feeling frustrated here ..."

Petite's eyes softened and she said, "I get that Hugo, listen you, we can fix this."

I looked at her and rolled my shoulders, loosening up. Yes, she was right, we could fix this. I'd been in worse situations before and sorted them. This was no different. Anyway, my complicated relationship with Cameron Bullard was something just waiting to explode. He had taken my house, and my brother had killed one of his nephews, which was not common knowledge, but I knew there were whispers. – and they were gaining ground. I could feel it in my shoulders, it was brewing up to boiling point. I could either wait until it blew up in my face, or take a hold and try to fix it. Cameron would go after my brother without hesitation, and even a secure, single cell wouldn't protect Douglas – Cameron's tentacles reach everywhere – and then he would come after me, as he knows I couldn't let my brother be killed without seeking vengeance.

"Yes, I need to fix it, Petite, and end this with Cameron once and for all."

My voice was strong, my head clear and focused. I had been on hold for months, waiting, waiting for this to blow up, and I was sick of it. I wasn't cut out for waiting. Petite looked at me again, the way she did when she wasn't sure about something I'd said.

"What?" I asked.

"What do you mean, '... end this with Cameron once and for all'?"

"I don't know, Petite, but there has to be some kind of closure here."

"I see..."

Petite fell silent. I could sense she was debating with herself whether or not to expand further on this. I hoped she would decide not to, simply because I would rather not go there just now. The moment passed. Petite flashed me a smile, chuckled and shook her head.

"You know, Hugo, both my mum and dad urged me not to start working for you."

I laughed – more of a bark really. Her father had told me this straight to my face. Fair enough, I'm pretty sure I would object too if one of my daughters wanted to work for a guy like me. That might sound somewhat old fashioned, but still, that was how it went.

"Can you imagine me working in a bank or something," she continued.

"No, and I'm glad you don't. I couldn't have built this business without you, Petite," I said sincerely.

Petite flashed a neat smile. "That's nice Hugo."

"You're welcome. How're your mum and dad anyway?"

I knew Petite's parents well. They'd lived in Spain for the last four years, running a pub and enjoying life. Peter Williams had been a successful Private Investigator who'd quit the game whilst on top and retired to the sun. Petite was their only child, a late-comer to the family. Gillian Williams, bless her, had struggled with the mother role, and consequently Petite had become independent early. But she still loved her parents, of course.

"Oh, they're doing well. I'm off to Spain next month to visit."

I liked the way she said that, supremely confident that this mess could, and would, be sorted by then, and life would go on. I took a sip of my coffee, trying to feel as confident as Petite sounded. Petite Williams was truly something, confident, smart, somewhat rebellious and totally without any personal angst. In comparison I was an ever-more growing bundle of emotional complexity – maybe I should be her assistant? The thought made me smile, which Petite noticed. As she looked up I was reminded of how utterly gorgeous she was too. For some reason, for which I was eternally grateful, we'd never become intimate. At times there had been a spark of sexual attraction, but neither of us had taken it any further.

"What Hugo?"

"Nothing, I'm just feeling grateful that I've got you. You keep me on an even keel, Petite."

I had said that a little too quickly. Feeling embarrassed, I felt my brow prickle with sweat. What a schmuck I was! A little flush appeared in Petite's cheeks. A moment of awkward silence followed before she waved it all away.

"Oh, stop it, Hugo! Let's focus."

"Yes, let's," I replied quickly, equally keen to move this on.

"Good! By the way, do you know who won the game?"

I shook my head. I didn't. My Sunday had been spent in here, ignoring the outside world with mobiles, internet and TV turned off, reading a good book. The protagonist appealed to me; I could relate to his problems and he kept me entertained. Stocked up on pizzas, non-alcoholic beer and off-grid for twenty-four hours, I was trying hard to give myself a rest from the disaster area that characterised my personal life.

Petite looked surprised, as she answered her own question, "Jens Brekken, that Norwegian guy. I think you did a job for him about two years ago – remember?"

I took a moment. Yes, I did remember Jens. Tall and blond, the type who could be on a poster for a Norway tourist ad; wholesome and healthy. I knew that wasn't quite the reality though. Snorting cocaine didn't quite fit the image, but that's what he was doing when I saw him last.

"Yeah, I remember him, the rebel son of the Brekken shipping magnate. I didn't work for Jens though, it was his father who'd hired me."

Jens was a gambler and international playboy, the type tabloids loved. Wherever Jens went, drama followed. My assignment had involved cleaning up and fixing the aftermath of a party that had gone totally overboard. It had taken some brokering skills and a decent amount of money to make sure no police or lawyers had become involved. Luckily, the party-goers were basically the same types as Jens; they all had a price. I then had to escort the wild man home to his father, Harald Brekken, patriarch of the family. Jens, although a few years older than me, behaved very much like a teenager suffering from inheritance-kid syndrome; privilege and easy-living had completely ruined any sense of decent character he may have once had. Jens wasn't pleased, but I got him home. The father had had enough, and the son was destined for a boot-camp-style rehab facility in Northern Norway, beyond the Arctic Circle. Staffed by a mix of medical professionals and Norwegian ex-special forces operatives, it was a pretty hardcore place, or so I'd heard.

"Right. Well, Hugo, rumour has it, he's cleaned up his act."

"Well, good for him! Snorting cocaine never was a good thing for sustainable health."

We both laughed. Although I could, in some way, relate to the world of Jens Brekken and his type, I never felt part of it, nor did I identify with it. My father was from a working-class background in Oslo and my mother was a well-born Scot; her family had been horrified when their relationship had become serious. The only reason some of her snobbish family came to accept this Norwegian into their inner circle was that he was a capable guy with money he'd made for himself. However, most of them didn't. My brother and I always identified with Dad, even though we didn't see much of him. Frank Storm was cool, really cool. When he came for the occasional visit to the posh private school where mother had stashed Douglas and me, we both absolutely loved it. This tall, blond guy with a brown leather jacket used to come to a screeching halt in front of the main building in a cool sports car. Then he would swagger into the place as if he owned it, smiling and laughing as he hugged us, not caring a jot who was watching. He had a strong presence, with his confident easy-going manner and his obvious capability. Following suit, Douglas and I also stood out, hence we fought a lot – Douglas, the brute that he was, more than me. He just loved fighting, I didn't as much, but I could handle myself and never backed down from a challenge. How I hated that school! I never forgave mother for dumping me there as soon as she possibly could ... anyway, I knew I needed to push those thoughts aside for now and investigate that poker game.

"I don't understand Julia's motivation. Why would she risk something like that?" mused Petite as she swung her left leg over her right. Her curvy frame was all female.

"Neither do I. Maybe she was in a sticky financial situation and felt desperate?"

I wasn't totally convinced about that. In fact, my words sounded outright wrong, even to my own ears. There were far less dangerous opportunities out there for Julia to make a quick buck, and the Julia I knew was smart. Petite also appeared reluctant to believe that rather thin hypothesis.

"No, I can't see that, Hugo. As far as I know she was financially sound and had built up a rather neat investment portfolio. There must be some other reason." Pausing for breath, she looked at me and added, "And you need to find that reason, Hugo."

"Time to hit the streets," I said, feeling the restlessness taking hold. I needed to get out on the street and start hunting. That was the way I operated best: getting out there, searching through the shadows.

"Yes. I'll start digging too. First though we need to clear your schedule."

Petite took charge. I didn't mind, she always kept me straight, and knew what could or couldn't be ditched. She wasn't only a premier hacker, but also an efficient business manager.

"Yeah sure, just tell me if there's something I definitely can't miss."

I might be in a mess, but then again, that was hardly new. There could be things on my schedule that only being in a coffin would be valid reason enough to skip. Petite took a moment to consider the entries for this coming week.

"Yes, you've got a meeting with Sir Ian Keller tomorrow at nine sharp – it's important. You can't cancel that, Hugo. Ian is important. We need the money, and besides, I'm getting a raise next month!"

Petite folded her hands in her lap and gave me a look that dared me to challenge her. I couldn't help but chuckle. I couldn't recall our discussing this, but never mind – she was a chancer!

"What did we agree on?" I asked, steeling myself for a financial blow.

"Oh, a modest 5% increase on the basic, starting from the first of next month. That's reasonable," Petite confidently announced.

And it sure was, I had expected ten percent, five was a bargain! I paid Petite well, and she was worth every penny of it; my business in all its shapes and forms was dependent upon her.

"Fine, that's a deal," I replied quickly, then moved on. "What does Ian want, it must have slipped my mind?"

Sir Ian Keller was an Edinburgh-based businessman, a tech entrepreneur and restless visionary type who always seemed to have a hundred projects going on at the same time. Super-smart, ruthless and hard-charging, he often attracted drama, which was good for me: Ian frequently needed problems fixed. We met a few years ago at a party and hit the right note straight away. I guess it was fair to say that on a personal level we liked each other.

"I don't know, Hugo, but you'd better attend. I know it's important, and that's that." Petite paused, giving me stern look before she continued, "You'd better tune in Hugo. I totally get that you've had a lot on your plate in the last few months, but now is the time to switch on ... you know that."

I looked directly at her and she held my stare. Normally I wouldn't respond well to anybody telling me to switch on, but this wasn't just anybody and she did have a point. I broke the stare, looked down, took a breath and told myself to pull it together.

Helena my current, but soon-to-be ex-wife had left me five months ago, as I'd had to give away our house to settle a stupid gambling debt. I couldn't blame her, it was me who had gambled and lost our home; I was responsible for this mess. She had taken our three little ones and gone down south to her parents, so I hadn't seen her or the kids for almost two months. On that last occasion her father, a powerful and wealthy man, had intervened, telling me in no uncertain terms to get lost. I had backed down and driven back up to Scotland. The last few weeks I'd been working on autopilot. What a mess! I had four children and used to pride myself on being a solid dad; the type who was there for the bad as well as the good, but now I was in the situation of not being able to see any of them. The two mothers of my children were both angry with me. I couldn't blame them for that, even if I tried; the anger I felt with myself was so intense sometimes it felt outright suffocating.

"Fair enough Petite, I've got to switch back on ... sorry to ask this, but have you talked to Helena recently?"

Petite looked at me with uncertainty, before turning away and shaking her head slightly. Taking a breath, she brought her focus back to me, her face a little flushed as she replied.

"That's something else we need to talk about. Something I've wanted to talk to you about, but couldn't find the right opportunity – might as well do it now."

I felt rush of mixed emotions racing through my body, this was embarrassing for us both.

"Hugo, I can't continue to be the broker or messenger or whatever I am, between you and Helena any more. You know – Helena knows – I love you both, and the little ones too, but it's not my place to be involved in this family situation. Surely you get that? Fair enough?"

"Yes, absolutely, it's not fair on you. I do apologise for this, Petite."

My voice was clear, part of me felt relief; this had been starting to put a strain on our working relationship. Petite's expression softened. I could see relief in her face too.

"Oh, don't, Hugo ... Let's just move on. I truly hope you and Helena can work this out." Petite stopped, searching I guessed, for appropriate words, but I used the interlude to take charge; it was about time I did so.

"Yes, you're right, let's move on. First point on the agenda is to find Julia. Father Black gave me seventy-two hours before, I suppose, this mess goes nuclear."

"You don't trust him, do you?" Petite asked.

"No, not at all, but I also doubt he would run straight to Cameron without having given me that time. Cameron would become livid, and nobody would want to be in his focus if that happened. But I worry about two possibilities: firstly, Cameron finding out from another source, and secondly, Angus blowing this whole thing up on an impulse."

"Agree. Nonetheless, either way you need to address this, Hugo; the clock is ticking!"

We sat for a moment chewing things over, then I sprang into action – it was time to get going.

Petite pointed to the door and said, "I'll start right away, Hugo, and I'll cancel my date tonight. You're gonna need all the help you can get."

"Thanks, I appreciate that Petite. Who was the lucky one?"

I shook myself into my black leather jacket. Shame about that, but personally I was pleased she'd be working her magic – on call to deal with whatever request I might have.

Petite shook her head. "Doesn't matter, just some French Masters student, who'll be disappointed, but nothing I can do about that."

I looked at her for a moment, sensing her vibe that I should leave this alone, so I did.

"Well, thanks again, will you start hacking everything you have on Julia, Father Black and ... and this Norwegian guy too? Text or email me anything and everything, and if you need me; I'm on ..." I paused and fished out my mobile. I had several, so I wanted to make sure Petite knew the right one to contact me on. She looked at the phone and gave me a nod.

"Right then, Hugo I'll get to work. You take care out there."

Petite gave me hug. At five foot four, she was a good six inches shorter than me. Her hug was lovely and so was her aroma, radiating a lush perfume that I gathered was new and had been for the benefit of her cancelled date. We separated and Petite smiled at me. I was reminded how close we were, true friends with nothing sexual in it; our relationship was platonic, the way it should be. It made our working relationship stable and solid.

"I always do. Call me." I said as I headed out of my office.

FOUR

As I hit the street, I took a deep breath of the moist Edinburgh air. A wind that had gained traction across the North Sea gave promise of a turbulent night ahead. Didn't matter to me, I was half Scottish, half Norwegian; miserable weather was ingrained in my spine. Looking up and down the street I knew I wasn't the only one. I needed time to clear my head and think. Being out and about was the best way to facilitate that. Just as I was about to walk, my mobile buzzed. I cursed the thing as always, but still answered. Without it I would be out of business. The caller's number had been withheld, as they often were.

"Hugo, is that you?" boomed the deep voice of Cameron Bullard, Edinburgh's most senior gangster boss. It stopped me in my tracks. With this morning's development in mind, I knew I had to tread carefully.

"Yes, Mr Bullard, it's me. How can I help you?" I forced myself to speak with a calm friendly tone, that of a man with nothing to hide, a man full of confidence.

"We need to talk. Tonight, at six at The Gravy."

It wasn't a request, but an order. Fear ignited deep down in me, but I was smart enough not to let it become overwhelming. Only true psychos and bluffers would claim never to experience fear. Even the most hardened combat soldier experienced fear, the key was how one dealt with it. With experience it was possible to learn how to channel it in the right direction and turn it from a disabler to an asset. Fear, when utilised correctly, could finely tune a person's instinct and provide incredible energy. Not to say it worked every time and didn't take its toll:

it did, and it had on me, but I could still work with it and move forward.

"You there, Hugo?" Cameron's obvious irritation jolted me back to the present.

"Sorry, Mr Bullard, the reception just broke up there. Of course, I'll be there at six, Mr Bullard."

"That's a good lad." Cameron terminated the call without further small talk.

I stood staring at the mobile screen for a moment, deliberating on why this gangster needed to talk to me. Would I be walking right into my own execution? There was no way to be sure, but that scenario didn't make much sense. I knew Cameron wasn't the type to spill blood on his own turf; he would assume that I'd taken the precaution of letting people know I was meeting him, and where. He knew that if I disappeared, enough noise would be made for the police to kick in the doors of his facility. The more I thought about it, the more certain I was. If Cameron wanted me dead, it would happen as far away from him and his patch as possible. Angus had given me seven-two hours, which I believed he would honour simply due to his desperation to find Julia.

I looked up at the darkening sky above Edinburgh and took solace in the gathering storm. It sharpened my mind. Then I did what I did best: let the promise of drama start my juices flowing. Let there be mayhem, I was ready! But first I needed food; my stomach groaned, and I was reminded that I hadn't eaten since breakfast. My blood sugar was dropping rapidly. To stay sharp, I needed fuel. There was this Italian down Leith Walk that dished out a mean pizza, heavily loaded with just about everything and spicy enough to burn itself down – just the way I liked it. I also liked the staff, and since the owner, Roberto, still owed me money, we'd come to an arrangement: I would eat for free until the debt was cleared. My office was only a ten-minute brisk walk away, so I decided to leave the car and go there on foot.

As I walked, I saw a young dad pushing a pram with pride. It made my stomach churn. Emily and Claire! My ex-wife and our daughter, my oldest child, were here in Edinburgh. Set aside the fact that Claire was still angry and had denied me contact with Emily, now they were, in my mind, suddenly vulnerable again. The trauma of six months ago, when Emily had been kidnapped in order to derail me from an investigation, was still fresh in Claire's mind. I knew that and I didn't blame her. Those had been the scariest days of my own life and had brought me close to a full mental meltdown. I don't care how strong a person claims to be, or how much of the mire they've been through, when your own kid disappears, fate unknown, it's a completely different ball game. Both Claire and Emily, as well as I myself, were still struggling with mental health issues. The thing about mental trauma is that time will often reinforce it, so that the negative impact on a person's mental well-being can become ever more severe. Post-Traumatic Stress Disorder had just proved that time didn't heal all wounds, particularly those that are unseen. Traumatised combat veterans, struggling to cope years after whichever war they had fought in, were living proof of this.

The more I thought about it, the quicker my stomach churned. Should I tell Claire? If I did, she would go ballistic and quite possibly take Emily and run. Would I then ever see Emily again? I allowed myself to curse as I took a big breath. Find perspective, Hugo, I whispered to myself, the way you did it when you were in the army. This was what I did, and I did it well. I would protect Emily and Claire without their knowledge, and complete my assignment to the point where, I hoped, normality could return.

Helena and our three little ones were away down in England. She would be at her parents, who lived in a mansion with excellent security. George, Helena's father, was well capable of looking after his family. I liked George and I knew he used to like me, but our relationship had taken a nose dive after the drama of six months ago. The father had sided with his daughter; fair enough, I would've done the same.

I needed to get things sorted and get on with it. The first thing was organising protection for Claire and Emily. I had a guy in mind: Thomas 'Tam' MacDonald, an ex UK Special Forces guy who now specialised in protecting people. He didn't fix problems as such, in the way that I did, but his protection service was world class. We knew each other well, we'd met when I served in the army, and we'd soon established a solid bond of friendship. We just clicked. He had been away on a job during Emily's drama, but I knew he was in town just now. I got his private number up and called him.

"Hugo, my favourite half-Norwegian, half-Scotsman. How are you?"

"I'm well. Listen, I'll get straight to the point here – I need a favour."

"Sure, name it." Tam wasn't the type to waste time.

"We need to meet face-to-face. Can you be at Bolt Senior in an hour?"

I needed to look the man in the eyes as I asked him this favour. A brief pause whilst Tam considered what I'd asked and checked his schedule.

"You got it – see you in sixty." Tam terminated the call without further small talk.

Bolt Senior was the code name we used for The Tap. My using it, and the fact that I hadn't given any indication over the phone of the favour I wanted, told Tam that whatever I needed was serious. Sixty minutes was just long enough for me to eat something and get over to The Tap.

I arrived at our meeting place before Tam and took a seat by the window. My mobile was in my leather jacket pocket, turned off, with the SIM card removed and placed in a small lead box I always carried. Likely over-the-top behaviour, but paranoia was my trusted, loyal friend. Besides paranoid guys lasted longer in this game than those who gambled unnecessarily, and I was finished gambling. The place was quiet with just a few heavy drinkers at the bar nursing their misery or whatever. I recognised all of them, and none rang any alarm bells. Charlie was away though. I didn't ask where – none of my business. The bar was attended by Jack, a dependable, stylish, late-twenty-something guy with an easy smile: characteristics Charlie valued.

Tam arrived with a couple of minutes to spare on the hour, bringing with him one of his operatives – a younger version of himself – fit, capable and serious. Tam quickly scouted the bar before his eyes settled on me. He shot me a quick smile and gestured towards the bar. I pointed to my coffee, so he got soft drinks for himself and his side-kick before coming over. Mini-Tam seated himself at a table between us and the rest of the bar, forming a sort of barrier against wagging ears. One of the punters at the bar looked over, met the eyes of Mini Tam, got the unspoken message and promptly returned to his beer.

"Good to see you, Hugo," said Tam.

He brought a black device from his jacket pocket, placing it on the table between our drinks. He pressed a button and the device began to make a low humming sound as he leaned back in his chair. Tam was a kit guy and possibly even more paranoid than me, which I found kind of comforting. I liked his tech passion. This was the 21st century after all – it was just a matter of time before robots fought wars and Artificial Intelligence presented challenges we couldn't even dream of. If you weren't ahead of the curve, you'd be behind it, and you'd lose. I looked at the machine and saw that it was a jamming device. If this place was bugged, the signal emitted from this little black box would completely drown our conversation. I knew Charlie regularly screened his place, but you never knew. That was a philosophy both Tam and I followed with discipline.

"What's up, Hugo. What's going on?" Tam fixed my eyes with his and waited.

I had decided not to hold back from him. Strictly speaking, he didn't need to know the reason behind the blackmail, but Tam was a smart guy, so he would soon work it out. Also, he needed to know I trusted him. I took a sip of the coffee, put the cup down and leaned forward.

"I need Claire and Emily protected for the next few days – maybe weeks – and I need that done without Claire being aware of it."

Tam knew them both, so when he'd learned about the drama of six months ago, he'd become livid because he hadn't been there to help. His expression hardened – both he and I were old school: women and children were absolutely off limits!

"Consider it done, mate. They still staying at that nice bungalow in Portobello?"

"Thanks, Tam. Yes, they're still there."

"What's his name – Bob or Bill – still there too?"

I laughed, "It's Tom, Tom Walker, and yeah, still the three of them." I felt a wave of gratitude flow over me – Tam and his crew were the real thing – I knew he'd help me.

"Okay then – you want to fill me in, Hugo?"

"Sure, I'm being blackmailed." I paused and watched as Tam raised an eyebrow. He didn't reply, just waited for me to continue. "This individual wants me to find Julia Felt, otherwise information dangerous to my life will be shared with another type who would be intent on causing me harm." I paused again, then took a sip of my now-tepid coffee.

"Well, that's unfortunate," Tam said, fixing his eyes firmly on mine. He continued, "Who is the blackmailer?"

"A Father Angus Black. Edinburgh Central Prison's most corrupt official. The man is a gangster and he's threatening to rat me out to Cameron Bullard. It's pure nonsense, but that doesn't matter; he has enough to make Cameron believe his story and put a contract out on me."

"You need nicer friends, Hugo!" Tam winked as he said this.

"Tell me about it. But this is part of my world Tam. I have to deal with it – and I will – but I need protection for Claire and Emily. I can't protect them whilst I'm sorting this out. I made a mess of things last year, and the tab for that is not yet covered. I cannot allow Claire and Emily to be hurt again."

Tam nodded; "Of course Hugo. I'm intrigued – this stuff is far more interesting than protecting wealthy and famous pompous arses. The money is ace, but the work is mind-numbingly dull. Nothing interesting ever happens. Anyway, sorry about that rant – so tell me."

"Well, you know Julia Felt? She's a poker player,"

"Yes. She's the UK number-one-ranked player."

"Well, she's gone missing and I'm being blackmailed into finding her, and fast!"

"Missing? But she played in the big game less than forty-eight hours ago." Tam leaned forward, his interest was keen.

"Were you there, Tam?" I hadn't expected him to know that. Leaning forward, I intruded into his personal space – such niceties forgotten in the intensity of the moment. His eyes remained focused on me, but in this close proximity, I couldn't fail to notice his weathered wrinkly skin, evidence of a life spent outside in all the elements.

"No, I wasn't, but Craig was. I had the evening off. What's going on here, Hugo?"

Rolling my shoulders, I glanced around. "I've got less than seventy hours to figure that out, Tam. Did Craig say anything had happened at that game?"

"Well, he said there was some drama between the player's bodyguards during the game." Tam paused to finish his drink. I was all ears. Impatiently, I tapped lightly on the table.

"Come on, Tam – tell me more."

"All right, you heard of a Bobby Traveller?"

"Crazy Bobby, gypsy hard man and full-on psycho? He's a legend in the Scottish underworld and a fully-certified nasty type."

"Right, so you know this guy is nuts. Half-way through the game he starts giving this Norwegian poker-player bodyguard a hard time. In his face, squaring up to him, hurling all kinds of abuse. But this guy doesn't bite. Just sits there, stone-faced. Craig was impressed. We don't know the guy, but he's apparently ex-Special Forces – but who isn't nowadays?" Tam broke a grin before continuing, "So, this guy's stone-cold calm, whilst Bobby's pitching himself further and further into a rage. The breaks are about to give and everybody's ready. Craig is armed but he can't let on about this in case the other bodyguard is too. Craig can see the guy's getting ready to respond to this lunatic's imminent attack. But then Mike Cunningham – you know who I mean? Well, he comes charging in with a baseball bat and after a brief, but crazy fight clubs down Bobby..."

"Yes, I know him – what happened next?" I was keen for Tam to continue.

"Mike's furious – he's in charge of the game security, and everybody knows Cameron Bullard doesn't tolerate any drama around his important events and venues. Anyway, while all this is happening, the game's ongoing in the main venue. This Bobby guy is knocked out cold but breathing as far as Craig can tell. Mike gets a couple of his guys to carry Bobby out. Then it's back to business – sitting around doing nothing – waiting for the game to finish. This Bobby guy never returns, and that's about it."

I took a moment to digest all of this, then asked, "Who was Bobby bodyguarding?"

"Julia Felt!" Tam raised an eyebrow for emphasis.

I was surprised because Julia and Bobby weren't a natural fit, even though they came from a similar background of mayhem and chaos. Julia was the type who'd worked and hustled herself away from the mire, whilst Bobby had positively embraced it. I was having a hard time imagining her approaching Bobby for his services; for starters, she preferred guys who not only had a full set of teeth, but who brushed them too.

"Do you know how that happened?" I asked, on the off-chance that Tam would know.

"How what happened?"

"How Crazy Bobby became Julia's bodyguard?"

Tam shrugged and shook his head, "No, Hugo, I don't, but Craig commented on that too. Julia's a stylish lady, but even if this Bobby guy won a million on the lottery, he'd still be an animal."

"All right, no worries Tam, but thanks for the info, appreciated." I smiled and drained my drink. A thought had just occurred to me, and it answered my question quite well.

"Guess, you have a theory, Hugo?" Tam's intelligent eyes remained on me and he grinned.

"Yes." I replied thoughtfully.

"I'm still intrigued – you want to share it?"

Tam was smiling but a certain hardness had entered his eyes. I took a moment to consider the situation; it would be easy to become paranoid here – not a totally unhealthy outlook to have – but I needed to trust Tam, and he needed to know that I did.

"Well, it isn't much really: Angus fronted the money for Julia to play and he provided the muscle as well. I know Angus has employed Bobby in the past and I'm assuming he made Bobby's use one of the conditions for forking out the money." In my mind that made perfect sense; I couldn't see Julia hiring Bobby herself. Unless I'd missed something, she definitely wouldn't have!

"Makes sense to me ... but there's more to this. More to this poker game. Right, Hugo?"

I took a breath and answered quietly, "Sure is, and that's what I need to uncover."

"If you need a hand, you come to me, okay? Anytime, you hear?" urged Tam, with genuine concern etched into his face.

"Thanks, and I will, but I need Claire and Emily protected, Tam. Whatever happens I can't let it hurt those two. I've caused them enough pain as it is."

"Right, I hear you, Hugo."

Tam broke a tight smile and glanced at Mini-Tam, who all this time had maintained a watchful silence, ensuring that our conversation had not been interrupted. He gave the slightest of nods in return. I guessed they needed to get on, and so did I. But first I wanted to know something. I leaned forward again.

"Before we go, Tam, who is the guy you protected at the poker game?"

Tam flashed a wide smile, as an amused sparkle glinted in his dark eyes. In hushed tones, he confided, "We're providing security and protection for this American businessman. He's here to inspect and promote his newly-bought Highland hunting estate. I think he fancies himself as a decent poker player too, as he bought himself a place at the table at a premium rate. He lost!" Tam chuckled before continuing, "The guy's a joke, Hugo. He's a completely vain inheritance kid – with an ego larger than the Atlantic Ocean and the mannerisms of a teenager who's overdosed on Godfather movies, which is hilarious considering he's sixty or something."

I laughed out loud.

"Honestly, Hugo – the guy's pathetic, a real-estate tycoon who's desperate to prove himself. But he pays extremely well and he loves being surrounded by tough guys, thinks it makes him look tough too! Loves hardware and all that, typical of a rich kid who's never served."

"You're actually working protection yourself?" I said with a smile, enjoying Tam's tale.

"It's all about the drama with this guy, Hugo. What we're doing is complete overkill, but this guy loves it – and we're charging him big time. Craig's the lead just now. Got to take turns – it's awful just being in his company."

"Well, good luck with that one." I glanced at my wrist watch.

"Don't need luck, Hugo, just patience like a mother with a crying toddler. I'd prefer a gun fight anytime!" Tam chuckled again before he continued, "Right – get back to me as soon as you can with your mission brief; by then we'll have Claire and Emily protected, and they won't even know it. Okay, mate?"

"You're my brother and I'm forever in debt to you." I said, extending my hand.

Tam's face had become serious. He'd already switched to work mode.

An hour later I was in my car, an Audi S8, a beast of a car, scrolling through the secure email Petite had sent me with information she had, so far, on Julia Felt. Petite was one seriously talented hacker and had started accumulating personal information on Julia. As I read it, gaps in my knowledge regarding this lady started to close up. I'd always considered Julia to be smart and careful, but what I read began to change my opinion. I saw that initially she'd been financially prudent. As she started to build her career, her money was invested in real estate. However, she became ambitious and started to lend to expand her portfolio, but then the crash of 2008 happened. Although the impact of this took a few years to hit home, when it did it hit her with a bang. I was starting to understand why she played poker with other people's money – she no longer had her own to play with. In reality Julia Felt looked like a debt slave, making enough to cover the interest payments, but never enough to clear her debts. That was not all, there were personal risks attached to playing with other people's money, and at times I gathered she would have to deal with very unhappy clients. I was totally engrossed as I read through the material Petite had accumulated, and I reminded myself not to unduly frustrate my very capable assistant. One document caught my eye. It was a personal contract template. It appeared to be legally watertight and stated that the investor agreed liability of between forty to one hundred percent of any potential loss. I bet Julia would get most investors to agree closer to one hundred percent liability than to forty percent. At the most, it appeared, she carried a sixty percent risk, so it wasn't a bad deal. Then again, Julia won most of her poker games. She would have to, just to keep the game going. But, crucially, she hadn't won this last one.

I was about to get up when my mobile buzzed. After checking the caller ID, I swiped the screen.

"Hugo, have you heard the news?" Petite asked, with a buzz to her voice.

"No, what's up?"

"A certain Jens Brekken, our Norwegian friend, has been found murdered in a car in Edinburgh." Her adrenaline was positively pumping through my phone.

"You're joking," I replied, knowing she wasn't.

"Well, Hugo, unless there's more than one Norwegian by the name of Jens Brekken in Edinburgh at this present time, then this is our guy."

"Tell me about it," I said as my brain went into overdrive.

"All right, I just got a text from a girlfriend of mine. She's a local reporter who's somehow made the scoop of her journalistic career. It's not been broadcast yet, but apparently this Brekken guy was found in the front seat of a car this a.m. in a back alley in Edinburgh. Killed, execution style, with a shot to the back of the head."

"Interesting," I replied. This was a game changer, a dramatic game changer. I didn't ask for her reporter friend's name, I'd get back to that if I needed to.

"Indeed. Have you read the email I sent you?"

"Not all of it yet, working myself through the attachments, reading as fast as I can. Very interesting reading though. What is it?" I asked.

"Well, to my surprise Julia Felt isn't financially secure; she's way over her head in debt!" Petite paused, she was obviously as surprised about that as I'd been. Julia had managed to keep this well hidden.

"Yes, I know, from what I've read so far, she's in trouble. Explains a lot, doesn't it? The successful façade was exactly that: a façade."

"Yes, so I guess it helped Julia when Jens transferred one hundred K to her, five days before the big game," Petite said.

I took a moment, one hundred K was one serious amount of money.

"Still not enough to join the game. Any indication of the transfer details?" I asked.

"The payment was made from a tax-haven holding company which is fully owned by Jens. The ownership details were hidden, but it's definitely him. I can dig more on that, but does it matter?" Petite paused, and I used the moment to say something that had just popped into my head.

"Jens was in on the fix ... Yeah, and I bet he fronted the money to the insider. Makes sense." I paused, it did make sense. How do you fix a game? Number one, there's always a risk it won't work out. I learned in the army that even the most carefully considered plan could fall apart when exposed to reality. Hence, one leveraged the risk. First, as a minimum, one needed an insider. In this case it had to be the dealer, but the dealer had to be careful, otherwise those outside the fix could become suspicious. Therefore, with two players involved it would be easier to guarantee the success of the fix.

"You're absolutely right, Hugo. Remember though there were initially two tables and the top-grossing two from those tables played the final game for the big pot. The insider had to be the dealer on the final table. They played this between them ..." Petite's voice was high-pitched, full of energy.

"Yes, do you know who the dealers were? As you correctly calculated, we need the name of the guy for the winner's table." My brain was now firing on all cylinders.

"I can't recall, but I'll find out. Okay, Hugo, so let's run with this scenario. How many do you think were involved?" Petite paused, scrambling to fit together the pieces of this puzzle.

"Mm, four minimum I guess: Jens, Julia, Angus and the dealer of the winner's table, who was also dealing at one of first two tables, I guess. Yes, another reason why there had to be two players, guaranteeing at least one getting through. What was the winning pot again?" I asked.

"So, initially two tables, twelve players all in, five hundred K minimum, and that's GBP Sterling. No refund, if you lost, you lost your five hundred K. Then there were two proper fat pigs who paid premium to play at the winning table, they paid two million each, so the winning pot was ten million. I'm pretty sure Cameron took a two million cut, leaving eight million for the winner. Nice pay day indeed ... How do you think they cut it, Hugo?"

I was impressed with the information Petite had already sourced, but then again, I shouldn't have expected any less, as Petite heard many whispers.

"Not fairly, not two million each. For starters, I'm pretty sure Angus wasn't considered in the finally tally – he was the designated fall guy anyway."

"Right, only problem is, he's now trying to make you the fall guy. And even though he didn't play himself, Cameron would go after the players involved too." That was Petite's take on it.

"True, but I think they hoped Angus would buy them time ..." My conviction was wearing rather thin. I now didn't have much trouble pairing Julia up with this, but why did Jens get involved? He didn't need money; his family fortune was vast. However, I remember the guy being a risk taker, an adrenaline junkie, one of those guys who jumped off things one shouldn't really jump off and who deployed the parachute at the last second. Nonetheless, it was one thing doing adventure sports, but quite another playing with dangerous gangsters. Could there be another reason? I heard Petite's breath too, she too was thinking hard, the whys and the wherefores still unanswered. There had to be somebody else playing here. Somebody else behind the scenes, pulling the strings. It still didn't make sense though.

"This is getting thin, Hugo," Petite finally said. I heard her take a drink before she continued, "Still, I believe this Jens fella was in on it, what do you think about the dealer?"

"I don't know, maybe he's still in on it, or perhaps he's started his own play. Either way, their plan is already falling apart. The body count has commenced ... and I have a pressing concern just now."

"You think Julia killed Jens?" Petite asked, matter-of-factly.

"Don't know, but guess we need to keep an open mind here."

"Yeah, we'd better. I'll find out who the dealer was and get back to you ... and what's your pressing concern just now?"

"Cameron just called me ... he wants to meet at six." I paused as I heard Petite take a sharp breath.

"No, you don't do that, Hugo. It might be a trap. You walk in, and that's it, you'll never walk out."

The concern in Petite's voice was touching, but I felt there was no choice, and anyway my gut instinct told me that wouldn't happen. Not now anyway.

"Petite, listen, I don't think so. If he was onto this already, I don't think he would've invited me, I'd just be picked up – end of. But if I don't go, then I'm pretty sure Cameron will unleash the dogs, so to speak ... I think right now we're ahead of this game. Just! Cameron doesn't invite people over to his family pub who he intends to have killed."

I paused and looked out of the front windscreen of the car as dark clouds gathered above Edinburgh. Symbolic in so many ways. Petite didn't say anything; she recognised the wisdom of what I was saying.

I cleared my throat and continued, "I need to see his eyes, I need to see the man and get a bearing on the land before this goes nuclear ... you sure you want to continue helping me here, Petite? I mean, this mess will turn bloody, it already has ... I wouldn't blame you if you wanted to bail out."

"No, no, Hugo, I'm on this! I'm not bailing out, we work together and that's that. I'll get back to you ... Do me a favour though ..." Petite replied quickly.

"Sure."

"Call Harry, tell me you will call Harry," Petite's tone was forceful.

"I promise, I'll call Harry," I said.

"Good, stay safe." Petite terminated the call before I could argue with her any more. I looked at the phone for a moment with immense gratitude, she truly was one in a million.

With my energy levels up, I didn't hesitate any longer, but reached for my phone again. I would definitely call Harry, but first I needed to make another call. I got up Detective Sergeant Chris Lafferty's number and hit the call button. DS Lafferty was a veteran detective in Police Scotland and one of the very few in the force who continued to have a soft spot for Douglas. Although he was a very capable detective, he'd been busted down the ranks a couple of times; the man was something of a maverick. That was probably why he had identified with Douglas, mavericks both, kindred souls and all that. I knew he'd been involved in a few shady deals during the years, nothing as serious as my brother, but then again Douglas must've been Scotland's dirtiest cop. It would take some effort to beat that. Chris and I had a good relationship, not the best of buddies, but he would allow me into the loop most times. Every Christmas I gave him an envelope and sometimes he got one under the table, depending on what I needed. And people wondered why I charged as much as I did. The running costs of Storm Consulting were very substantial.

After a few rings my call to Chris went onto voicemail; I terminated the call without leaving a message. What was this: do-not-answer-Hugo-Storm's-calls day? I allowed myself to mentally curse Chris Lafferty. I needed somebody to curse just now, and Chris in his absence, would do.

FIVE

The Gravy was Cameron Bullard's nickname for his favourite family pub, The Falcon. Why he called it The Gravy, I had no idea. It was one of several establishments he owned in Edinburgh, and was a large family pub. Being a father of six and a grandfather of seven at the last count, Cameron classified himself as a family man. He was the type to conduct business in hushed conversions in the back booth whilst his kids came and went. Not that this made him a soft touch in business; those who made that mistake did so at their peril. His crew was more loyal than most crime outfits. If you proved your loyalty and commitment to Cameron, then he would look after you, no matter what. I knew he liked me, always had, regardless of whatever debt he may have owed to my dad, and I had to admit that a part of me liked him too. I suspected part of the reason was that we considered each other to be loyal family men. 'If you cannot be trusted to look after your own family, how can I trust you?' was one of Cameron's favourite sayings.

Being Cameron Bullard, he was also paranoid, with good reason. He had served time, but considering his life-long criminal activity, his time spent behind bars had been limited. Cameron was a difficult individual to prosecute, his security was top notch and always under review. He had numerous successful legitimate businesses, built up over the decades, and his involvement in criminal activity was so hands-off it was almost impossible to prove. Still, Cameron was a very dangerous man. If you did him wrong, you disappeared, never to be found again. So, although I kind of liked the man, I never forgot that Cameron wouldn't hesitate to have me killed if I crossed the line, solid family man or not.

I entered the pub with a minor ache in my abdomen. That was okay, my hands weren't clammy; in fact I felt confident – not arrogant – just calm and confident. I'd been in enough sticky situations to know how to handle fear, anxiety and stress. Only actors in the movies and real-life bluffers claimed not to feel stress. It was all about management of those emotions and channelling that energy in the right direction. A smart operator used that energy to his or her advantage.

The Falcon was a busy place, large and fairly well decorated, though a little tacky for my clean Nordic taste, but everyone to their own. I was noticed within seconds, and a serious young man approached me. He was a little younger than me, but had the cold eyes of somebody at home with violence.

"May I help you?" The guy's politeness surprised me, but then again Cameron was a stickler for manners. I knew one of his mantras was that being a thug was no excuse for lacking in manners. Many people, me included, found that funny, but not to his face mind you! He dealt with a steady stream of business contacts daily, many legitimate, so his goon squad had to know how to behave.

"I'm here to see Mr Bullard. Tell him it's Mr Hugo Storm," I said, as I scanned the pub, keeping it formal just for the heck of it. I recognised several faces, and a few nodded in acknowledgement. I nodded back.

"Right, Mr Storm, just wait here," the guy replied after giving me a quick once-over. Another huge guy, a veritable muscle mountain, stepped forward as the first guy turned and disappeared into the back of the pub. I looked at the muscle mountain – I remembered the guy. He was one of the thugs who'd clipped off one of my brother's fingers during the big drama of six months ago. He'd paid for it though, that nose would never be straight again. He surveyed me without any visible emotion, and with no effort to make small talk, which was fine by me. After a few minutes the first guy returned.

"Follow me," he said, as he started walking towards the back of the pub.

I did so, as the muscle mountain stepped to the side. Cameron was sitting alone in a shielded booth in the back. In front of him was a laptop, which he closed as I slid onto the bench opposite. A couple of leather-bound note pads lay on his left side and a coffee mug on his right. A mug of steaming hot coffee was right in front of me, black, just the way I liked it. Cameron took off his glasses and nodded towards the mug.

"Americano, they call it nowadays. Black coffee, we used to call it. No sugar."

"Thank you, Mr Bullard," I replied, and looked at the laptop.

"Liam, my six-year-old grandson, wants a laptop. His dad, my son Davie, a knucklehead, says no, so the young lad comes straight to me. I like that, the lad's got initiative and is smart. Very smart. What do you think I should say, Hugo?" Cameron waited, his intelligent eyes burning through mine.

I looked at the man, and took a moment, "Say yes. Kids nowadays will grow up with technology in every aspect of their lives. There'll be two types of people: those replaced by it and those controlling it." I took a sip of my coffee.

Cameron smiled and leaned back. He stroked his silver hair with his meaty hand. Not particularly handsome, but a man radiating confidence and authority. His potential for violence was evident – even a fool could sense that.

"See, that's why I like you, Hugo: you're a straight shooter ..." He paused, and the smile disappeared.

"You are a straight shooter, aren't you, Hugo?"

"Yes, I am, Mr Bullard."

I held his stare and nodded. My tone was confident and relaxed, but that was not the way I felt inside. However, it was how I dealt with tension, not letting it take charge. If the day ever came when it did, then that would be the time to quit. A tense silence fell, as Cameron considered whatever he had in mind. The intensity of his stare continued, and

I felt moisture starting to form at the base of my neck. I managed to keep my facial expression neutral and unaffected by what was going on in my head. I considered it time to name-drop Harry.

"What's up Mr Bullard? I've got Harry waiting outside and he's yanked up his rates."

I was letting him know I had an insurance back-up. Harry was a retired police officer, who ran an Edinburgh-based chauffeur company, using two top-end executive saloons. One of his speciality services was to take people to sensitive meetings and make sure they came out again afterwards. If his client didn't return as arranged, there were no dramatic gun-slinging entrances by him, but Harry could be guaranteed to call his buddies in the police. He carried enough goodwill and power to trigger a rapid raid of the place. Cameron knew Harry and his speciality service. He grinned and shook his head.

"What're Harry's rates nowadays?"

"Too high!" I replied simply, keeping the grin on my face. Just a small grin, mind you. It wasn't wise to get too chummy with Cameron. It was quite one thing for him to crack a joke, but he didn't necessarily tolerate anyone else's attempts at humour.

"You worried you wouldn't come out afterwards, Hugo?" Cameron laughed.

"I worry about everything, Mr Bullard. Needed a driver anyway."

Cameron looked at me and nodded. Another silence commenced. I waited. Cameron gently moved his laptop away and leaned forward with his hands folded together on the table.

"Okay, we've agreed you're a straight shooter. Then you'll help me out with this little problem. Yes?"

"Of course, Mr Bullard," I replied with a confidence I didn't have.

"Right, it appears something dramatic has happened to a Norwegian citizen, a man called Jens Brekken."

"Yes, I know!" I answered abruptly and to the point. Another rule of mine: don't talk if there is no need to. Talking too much could just compound trouble. Cameron looked at me knowingly. It wasn't news yet, but Cameron knew I heard things before they became common knowledge. It wouldn't sit right if I claimed not to know; it would make Cameron wonder why, and that was never good.

"You knew this lad, didn't you, Hugo?"

"Well, I knew him of him, Mr Bullard, not as a personal friend though."

Cameron arched an eyebrow and took a sip of his coffee. Then he just looked at me, silently waiting – classic trade craft that causes the other party to develop doubt. It was working. The little voice of doubt at the back of my brain was telling me that he knew more than he was saying. Cameron had a life time's experience of shady, tense negotiations. In fact, everything was a negotiation to Cameron, even a police interview. But I wasn't an amateur, and I was telling the truth, so far anyway. Jens Brekken wasn't a friend of mine.

"Right, but you did know him?" Cameron kept pushing.

I took another sip of my coffee, buying myself some time. Where was he going with this? And how forceful should I be in the distinction between friend and acquaintance?

"Mr Bullard. I knew of him," I answered in a friendly manner, but with emphasis on of.

Cameron Bullard seemed to be debating with himself before he moved on. I had stood my ground, and that was important. Show weakness to a wolf, and he will strike you down without hesitation.

"Okay, Hugo, I get the distinction. He played in my game for less than forty-eight hours before his untimely end. That is no good." Cameron's tone had turned icy.

I nodded my agreement regarding the unacceptability of that situation. Even though I really didn't like where this was heading, I had no choice but to stay. I knew there was no chance of my walking out of the pub unless Cameron said I could. I noticed two of his goons, one being the muscle mountain, moving in closer. I had Harry outside, but I guess

Cameron could deal with that if it came to it. It depended on how angry he was. I glanced at the goons, broke a tight grin and focused back on Cameron. He stared at me, his face neutral. I couldn't read his vibe. My tongue was in the process of gluing itself to the top of my mouth – I could feel the tension rising. I forced myself to relax, and mentally prepared myself to fight. I wouldn't go easy, they would have to work for it. Cameron was still looking at me, I was pretty sure he couldn't sense my tension. I had always been good at hiding that. Then he pointed at me and asked in an icy tone.

"Tell me, when did you last see this Jens Brekken?"

SIX

"I was just about to make the call, Hugo!"
Harry raised his right eyebrow in a conspiratorial kind of way as I slotted myself into the front passenger seat. I glanced over and shook my head.

"Well, it took a bit longer than anticipated, Harry. No worries. Do you mind dropping me off at 39, St. Andrew Square?"

The relief I felt was immense, but I wasn't about to dwell on it. And although Harry was fishing for info, if nothing but for sheer curiosity, I wasn't going to share anything with him. He didn't know why I'd gone to see Cameron in the first place, so I certainly wasn't about to tell him now. That was how it worked, and Harry understood that.

"Sure thing!" Harry drove off, not at all offended by my lack of communication.

I settled back in the comfortable seat of the Mercedes S-class that Harry was driving. The journey would only take about ten minutes, but that was long enough for me to reflect on what I'd learned in my face-to-face meeting with Cameron. Basically, he was keen to understand any potential financial repercussions to himself, following Jens Brekken's dramatic death. A damage control exercise had commenced. The good news was that, so far, I wasn't prominent in his consideration. He'd been satisfied with my, honest as it was, denial of any involvement in that murder. However, the bad news was that Cameron Bullard was now on the hunt himself. I was certain that sooner or later he would start to realise that the game had been rigged. He already knew it'd been compromised, the winner robbed and murdered less than forty-eight hours after it'd finished; something was obviously wrong.

Cameron viewed this as a direct challenge to himself, and his authority. Obviously, I had considered the possibility of Cameron being behind the murder, but that didn't make any sense. Why would he do that, only to attract heat from the police, as well as bad publicity? That would be the worst business practice I could think of, and Cameron Bullard was a business man – a successful one. After talking to him, I had discarded that scenario. But I knew one thing, the impetus for me to find Julia was now even greater, so my first port of call was Bar 39, a swanky bar in the city centre, where the hip and wealthy of Edinburgh ventured. I checked my phone again to see if my earlier text had been answered – yes, at Bar 39 a person of great interest to me was currently waiting.

Just at that moment, Harry brought the big Mercedes to a halt outside the bar. I turned towards him and shook his hand. "Thanks Harry, much appreciated, just email Petite with the bill, and she'll pay straight away."

"Of course, and take care, Hugo. Don't hesitate if you need me again." Harry gave me a knowing look.

"Will do," I replied as I took a breath of the moist air and looked around. The gathering storm had fizzled out to pretty much nothing and the evening now gave the promise of something rather pleasant. But this was Scotland, and I knew that could rapidly change. The weather in Scotland often likes to play pranks, to trick you into believing that something nice is coming and then hit you square in the face with something very unpleasant just a short time later. Much like my life really.

I walked straight up to the front door, by-passing the queue, which raised a few shouts of protest from some, until I shot them a hard look. The murmuring continued, but I ignored it.

"Evening Hugo," said Derek, one of the two well-dressed bouncers working the door, as he lifted the thick rope blocking the entrance and let me through.

"Good evening Derek." I responded, nodding to his side-kick, a younger guy who I didn't recognise.

The '39 was busy as usual, good-looking people everywhere with money to burn, and energy to do so with gusto. Know this, rich people like to party and they also like to mingle with their own kind. The prices in the '39 were outrageous, even from a Norwegian point of view, and that said something, but it meant the crowd all had money. I took a minute looking around as I walked into the main area, where a free-standing central bar was predominant in the big room. A quartet of hip-looking, smoothly efficient, bartenders served the punters, who were buying over-priced booze and cocktails. A couple of people I knew nodded and said hello. I returned their greetings. The noise was such that I couldn't hear much of what they were saying, which was just as well, I wasn't there to socialise. I walked around, scanning the quieter areas of the bar, and made eye contact with the person I was looking for.

"Hello, Hugo, how are you?" Sheila Collins' smoky voice greeted me. She was perched on a stool in a corner of the bar, next to a big guy, literally watching the money rolling in.

"I'm fine, Sheila, how are you?"

Politely, giving a gentle touch to his shoulder, Sheila asked the big guy, "Do you mind giving us a minute, Stan? I just need to talk to my good friend, Hugo."

Stan flashed me a warning look, but I didn't bite. He was just another of Sheila's boyfriends – a toy-boy – he'd probably be gone in a few months' time, replaced by another stud of her choice. Why not? Sheila lived her life as she wanted, not the way other people or society thought she should.

"No problem, Sheila, I need to make some checks anyway," said Stan, in an American accent. Sheila's obvious amusement sparkled in her eyes. Stan's attempt to inflate his own importance had not fooled her, nor me.

"You do that, Stan," she replied and flashed him a smile. Stan's tanned, chiselled face flushed, and he scurried away, almost like a scolded puppy with its tail between its legs.

"I think your Stan boy is a bit upset."

Sheila laughed, "Oh, Stan's just fine. He can handle being teased, Hugo."

"Really? I'm not too sure about that. Anyway, you dating Americans now? What's wrong with the Scottish studs?" I continued with fake disgust in my voice.

"Funny ... not ... stop it, Hugo! You make me sound like a really horrible person. And that's not who I am – you know that."

Sheila leaned over towards me and gave me kiss on the cheek. Her full lips were tender on my skin, her perfume was gorgeous. Our eyes met. Sheila was in her mid-forties, and a life of late nights and excessive alcohol and cigarettes was starting to leave its mark. But she was still a beautiful woman, who radiated a vibe of warm joyfulness.

"Sorry Sheila, I'm just standing up for the local boys," I chuckled.

Sheila held my gaze and laid a hand on my thigh. Just a simple touch but it was electric nonetheless, an utterly sensual feeling – my mouth went suddenly dry.

"Hugo, what are you talking about? Is this why you wanted to see me?" Her voice was smokier than ever.

I shook my head and explained, "I'm afraid not. I'm here to ask you about Julia Felt."

My tone was friendly, as inwardly I fought to suppress the warm feeling her hand was giving me. I didn't have to fight for long; at hearing my words Sheila removed her hand, and instantly her face lost its softness. She took a sip of her drink, slowly swirled the ice cubes around in her glass, and stared challengingly at me.

"What about Julia?"

Her voice sounded edgy and defensive, and I was reminded the lady was no fool. She was a ruthless business woman, nobody's victim, and Julia's best friend. Slowly lifting my hands in a calming gesture, I tried to appease her.

"Sheila, I'm here as a friend. You know me, and you know I wouldn't hurt Julia." I became aware that Stan had reappeared behind me and I could sense his fury straining to be released. I knew he was angry with Sheila, but would be more than happy to take it out on me. He would lose, and badly. I glanced over my shoulder and gave him a cold look. With my eyes fixed on him, I spoke again, "Sheila, you want to tell your boy here to go away?"

I held Stan's eyes; he gave in first. Looking down, he quickly lost courage, and I knew the toughness was pure façade. This was an Instagram gladiator, a twenty-first-century virtual hero with all bluster and no show. Sheila waved him away with an annoyed look and focused back on me.

"Okay, Hugo I hear you …" Sheila paused, checked for wagging ears, then continued, "Who asked you to look for her?"

"I'm looking for her myself, but I'm not the only one, Sheila. Trust me when I say that I am, without doubt, the guy Julia would prefer found her first!"

Sheila's face lost some of its lush colour and I saw the worry in her eyes as she looked back at me, taking a moment to consider what I'd said. Then she gestured for another drink, obviously feeling the need for something to calm her nerves.

"Point is, Hugo, I don't know where she is either. Haven't heard from her since Friday last." The worry in her voice sounded genuine, but the vibe I picked up told me she was lying.

"You know about the poker game?" I asked after thoughtfully considering my next step. She would, as she used to be a poker dealer by trade. Sheila nodded as she took a drink from one of her hip, female bartenders, then waited until she had returned to serving the many others queuing around the bar.

"Yes, and I asked her not to play. She didn't like that, but nonetheless, I'm sure she didn't play just to spite me. There was another reason, unknown to me ... What do you know, Hugo?"

"Why did you ask her not to play?"

Sheila considered my question for a moment, annoyed I hadn't answered hers.

"Because Julia shouldn't be associated with the likes of Cameron Bullard. She doesn't need that, and I told her so, in no uncertain terms ..." Sheila's voiced trailed off, she shook her head and looked down. I didn't say anything, my instinct told me she was playing a game here.

"Now, Hugo, tell me, what do you know?" Sheila said and looked at me intently. I took a moment to process before I replied.

"Your advice was sound, something went very wrong at that poker game ..." I checked that no-one was listening before continuing, "The winner was killed at some point after the game had finished in the early hours of Sunday."

I studied Sheila's shocked reaction. If she was faking this, then she was a great actress. All the signs were there of somebody genuinely surprised. She hadn't expected that.

She pulled herself together quickly and asked, "Who was the winner?" Her voice was cool and composed.

"A Norwegian guy called Jens Brekken – heard of him?" I decided I was going to play along.

"Yes, I think so, he was here in Edinburgh a few years ago, a flamboyant character, hard to miss really, as I recall ... didn't you clean up his mess one time, Hugo?"

"Yes, but that's not relevant here."

Sheila studied me for a moment before she replied, "Okay, so what now, Hugo?"

I was about to say; you tell me, instead I replied "I need to find Julia – and quickly ..." I paused, took her left hand in my right and looked her straight in the eyes. "Do you trust me, Sheila?"

She didn't immediately reply, and I knew she was debating with herself, buying time I guessed. For what and who?

"Why do you ask that?" Sheila finally replied, withdrawing her hand from my grip.

"Because I am asking you this: will you let me know if Julia contacts you, or if you get any information from anyone else? Will you let me know?" I knew she wouldn't, but she wasn't the only one buying time.

"Are you telling me you won't have Petite hacking me the minute you leave, if she hasn't already?"

There was no anger in what she had said, just a statement of reality. I ignored her insinuation, got off the bar stool, fished out a business card and laid it on the bar next to her drink.

"Please tell Julia to contact me, sooner rather than later. This is getting nasty, Sheila, and fast!"

Sheila looked at me for what seemed like an age, before she picked up my card and silently read the numbers. Then she put it back down and took a sip of her drink.

"All right, Hugo, if I hear anything, I'll let you know, and if Julia does contact me, I'll tell her to get in touch with you. Fair enough?"

"Thank you," I said, extending my hand.

"Stay safe Hugo." She gave me a tired smile and shook my hand lightly.

As soon as I hit the street, I called Petite. From her tone of voice, I knew she must have been pacing with worry.

"Hugo, I've been worried."

"Yes, I'm fine, thanks. Anyway, listen, I need you to hack anything and everything relating to Sheila Collins."

"Already have – well, still in the process of. She's one of Julia's best friend, so I thought it made sense."

I allowed myself to laugh, of course Petite would do that.

"Anything?"

"No, not yet, but I'm still digging. You sound keen Hugo, what's going on?"

"I think Sheila is involved."

"Wow, that's interesting, do you think she might be the dealer?"

"Yes, but I need that confirmed."

"That won't be a problem. How did it go with Cameron?"

"I got out in one piece – guess that could be deemed as success, of a sort." I'd started walking, and looked around before I continued speaking,

"Cameron knows Jens is dead, his contacts in the police must've informed him. He's not pleased ... I've really got to find Julia before he does." I said this more to myself than to Petite.

"It was just a matter of time before Cameron knew, Hugo, you know that. But you're right, you've got to find Julia, and quick."

"Anything else, Petite?" I felt a little annoyed – she was a smarty pants sometimes!

"No, not just now. I'll keep digging and get back to you. You keep me up-to-date too." Petite knew I didn't like being ordered around, but I guess she thought that excluded her.

"Will do, Boss," I replied and terminated the call.

SEVEN

The walk through Edinburgh city centre cleared my head. This city always filled me with positive energy, despite the drunk who tried to pick a fight with me as I walked through the streets. Being part of a group made idiots feel brave. The drunk, a large dude with angry red face and urine-stained trousers, was persistent for a moment; I had to stop and give him a look. His friends, less drunk, recognised that he was about to make a bad mistake, and pulled him away. Some people drink too much, and then just can't help themselves; the alcohol brings out the worst in them. I had to chuckle as I watched the guy being pulled away, his four friends dragging him along clearly against his will. Then I turned and walked on, heading towards my car. Fifteen minutes later I slotted myself behind the steering wheel, turned the engine on, looked up at the sky and watched as dark clouds were starting to gather above. Where had they come from? But then again, what else was new? I got my mobile out; it was time to make another call.

Mike Cunningham was my premier informant within the Bullard crime family. I'd saved Mike's life once, got him out of trouble a couple of other times and provided him with a deposit for his secret, offshore, bank account now and again. Mike had a plan, which was to escape to the sun and enjoy a peaceful life once the offshore bank balance had reached a satisfactory level. It was fair to say the man was a reluctant informer. I had sworn to him that none of the information he provided me with would end up with the authorities. Nonetheless, we both knew there wouldn't be any future sun and cocktails if Cameron ever discovered our arrangement. This bothered Mike at times, but his personal debt to me helped to subdue those worries, as did my contributions to his retirement fund.

"Hello," Mike's sleepy voice finally answered.

"It's Hugo. You sleeping, Mike?" I checked the time. It was just before eight in the evening – working hours for types like Mike.

"I was before you called and woke me up. What's up?" His voice sounded hoarse, and he started to cough.

"I just had a meeting with your boss, and he wasn't very happy. Why on earth didn't you warn me?" I feigned anger, my voice suitably spitting fire.

"What? What're you talking about?" Mike's voice was now clear and sharp. The man had snapped fully awake. Then again, hearing that there was some information Mr Bullard wasn't happy about would make every single one of his crew stand up and pay attention. Particularly a guy who was essentially a rat.

"What do you know about Jens Brekken, the Norwegian poker player?" I asked.

Pushing on, I was asking an open question as I wanted to see how Mike would react. I paid this guy for information, but it was more for leverage really. Paying Mike meant I had him, I owned him and therefore could play him. In theory anyway.

"What about him, Hugo? He won the flamin' game – what more is there to say? What exactly is going on?" The alarm in Mike's voice was now palpable.

I wanted to ask him directly if he'd been involved, but instead I said, "You tell me, Mike."

A silence followed, whilst Mike tried to figure where I was going with this. I heard some noise that sounded like he was getting out of bed. Why was he in bed as this time? I waited. A burp came through my phone, followed by Mike's now very tense and angry-sounding voice.

"No, you tell me, Hugo!"

Now it was my turn to take a minute. I had hoped that springing this on him out of the blue would make him provide valuable information of some sorts. But he wasn't an amateur; if he was involved, he wasn't going to tell – groggy or not. Nonetheless, I didn't give up. Mike had been there at the poker game, and my gut told me he knew something. I wanted to find out if he had killed Jens or had been involved in some other way. Mike was one of Cameron's senior guys, and I knew he'd killed for him in the past.

"Jens Brekken is dead and Cameron is furious." I paused and focused solely on listening. When taken by surprise, people with something to hide will sometimes change their breathing pattern. It wasn't an exact science, but just now I needed any clue I could gather. Linking Jens' death with Cameron's anger was another way of tightening the screw.

"Where's this coming from?" Mike's voice was now stone cold, and I just knew he had somehow been involved. But in what capacity? Was he involved together with Julia? Was he freelancing? Was he working for Cameron? Had I been wrong about Cameron? Did he already know the game had been rigged and was now seeking vengeance? Maybe he'd let me walk out earlier so I could lead him to Julia? The questions were multiplying by the minute. And regardless of the debt Mike owed me, or the money I paid him, he wasn't going to tell me. But I pushed on, knowing I'd be able to pick up important information by reading between the lines and by what Mike didn't say.

"I don't know where Cameron got this from, but that's what he told me. And, as I said, the man is angry."

I paused and listened. Mike did the same. We were like a couple of chess players trying to outmanoeuvre each other, waiting for the other player to make a mistake. Mike, by now, had realised what my game was, and I in turn had realised that he was on to me.

"So, what are you saying?"

"I'm not saying anything, Mike. Just wanted to know why you didn't warn me," I replied, trying another angle. If I could make the man angry, he might slip and say something of value. Angry people make mistakes.

"Warn you about what, Hugo?" Mike's icy tone confirmed that he was aware of my tactic. I decided to round it up for now – but I'd definitely be keeping Mike on my radar.

"Okay, Mike. Listen, I've just got out the lion's den in one piece. I thought you should've warned me, but I realise now that's not fair. I'm sorry mate." I wasn't sorry, but there was no point in aggravating this situation any further.

The play hadn't worked, so I needed to defuse the tension, but I was fully aware that might not work either.

"Right, I hear you, Hugo. I'll see you later." With that Mike hung up.

I dropped my phone on the passenger seat beside me and mulled over what'd been said. There was one interesting piece of information I'd got out of this: Mike had been sleeping. He wasn't one of your nine-to-five working stiffs; not the kind of guy who got up at six and sorted out his lunch box before commuting to the office. Evening time was working time for guys like Mike. Therefore, I presumed he must've been awake all night and much of the morning too. Interesting.

"What have you been up to, Mike?" I whispered to myself as I slotted the gear lever into drive.

EIGHT

Julia was well connected and heard the whispers in the shadows just as clearly as I did. If this then created more challenges, would she go deeper underground, or would she reach out to discover why I was looking for her? I guessed that would depend on who she was hiding from in the first place. This obviously related to the poker game. The winner was dead, and the money had disappeared. So, this was a robbery, plain and simple. It made sense. The most logical question in this chain concerned Julia's potential involvement in the killing of Jens Brekken, a scenario I would have dismissed less than twenty hours ago, but maybe not now. So, following on this chain of thought, if she had been involved in the killing of Jens, then why? Had she become greedy and decided not to share with him? The allure of a cool eight million could test the integrity of even the most moral individual, causing them to step over the line. Outward signs of virtue are one thing – hard cold cash is something very different. Maybe the killing wasn't part of the plan she thought she'd signed up to? Complicated plots often turned sour, particularly when big money was involved. Being acquainted with somebody was very different from knowing how their mind worked. My trade craft was unlocking personal secrets, and I would need to do that with Julia Felt.

My mobile buzzed again, breaking my focus. I reached out and saw that it was a text from Petite: 'It's hitting the news, local and national, at nine. And a Detective Sergeant Rachel Muller from Police Scotland has called, she wants to talk to you. I gave her your 655 number. Take care.'

Petite was referring to one of my other mobiles, I had several. Some official, others not. One's whereabouts could be tracked with surprising ease in today's world and I frequently needed to be untraceable. The mobile in question was in the glovebox of my car, switched off, with the SIM card in a small lead box. I brought it out, slotted in the card, switched it on and checked the voicemail. The voice of D. S. Muller was pleasant enough, but good detectives are careful not to create alarm in people they want to speak to. The best ones can easily smooth talk a potential suspect straight into cuffs. I laid the phone back on the seat and took a moment. This was complicating matters, but I couldn't dodge this detective for long, unless I wanted even more heat on myself. Another scenario was forming as I sat thinking hard, and it wasn't a pleasant one. Was I, somehow, a fall guy for the murder of Jens Brekken?

From yesterday morning to this morning I'd been alone in my now-combined office/flat. I had tried to tune out of my personal mess and had immersed myself in a good book that'd been gathering dust on one of my bookcases. A great crime tale. I enjoyed the protagonist, a cool character with the sort of personal issues I could relate to. Now this presented a problem, if the police demanded an alibi: Mickey was a fictional character, so he couldn't much vouch for my whereabouts!

I allowed myself to curse Father Angus Black. If this was part of his doing, then he would pay. I tapped a rhythm on the steering wheel; in fact, he was going to pay regardless. There wouldn't be any happy ending here. Even if I did provide him with what he wanted, he wouldn't just shake my hand, solemnly promise to bury this information away for good and part company with me as good chums do. No way. I would never trust him, and he would know that. Why was he gunning for me? I guess there were plenty of reasons. But maybe the stars were aligned in a certain way and the beam hit me as the perfect fall guy? If I was being set up, I was confident I could walk. But, with the slow machinery of law enforcement involved, it would take time, and time just now was a critical factor.

I needed to stay free and mobile for the next seventy-odd hours, and not be sitting in a holding cell awaiting the good people of Police Scotland to clear my name. I was applying my worst-case-scenario thinking here, if you think it might go wrong, assume that it will. I needed an inside track on this before I contacted the police detective who was trying to get hold of me, and who I couldn't remember having any history with. A thought hit me, and using my other mobile I quickly texted Petite, asking her to do some digging on this D. S. Rachel Muller.

A news bulletin on the radio caught my ear and I turned up the volume. It was local Edinburgh radio and the news presenter was fully charged as he reported the story. A Norwegian man had been found dead, Police Scotland had confirmed, at an undisclosed location in Edinburgh city. That was basically it. The news presenter didn't have much more to go on, but nonetheless he gamely tried. The pride in his voice that this news story had been broken by one of their reporters was obvious. I continued to listen but there wasn't much more. I knew this was just the start and the story would soon grow legs. Last year there had been just over fifty murders in Scotland, most involved domestic situations or drug-and-alcohol-related, spur-of-the-moment killings. They were usually messy, amateur stuff the police would solve fast, very few involved guns and even fewer were professional-type hits. This particular murder would blow up, for sure, and that meant the police would feel the heat themselves and thus throw everything they had at it. That was bad news for me if I was being framed, as they would soon come after me with gusto.

I needed to talk unofficially with somebody inside Police Scotland who could tell me if I was a person of interest, a suspect, or wanted in some other capacity. I rang Chris Lafferty again. It rang out before the voicemail kicked in. I didn't leave a message. There was no point trying to read anything into that. I would try again later.

"Focus back on Julia," I mumbled to myself. I had decided Julia would definitely be informed that I was looking for her. Sheila, for one, would let her know – if she could. So, I spent a few minutes deciding what my approach should be, and the answer was to keep it simple. From my days in army intelligence, I knew the best way was the simple way. I would go looking for Julia, and only for myself. I would not mention Angus, there would be nothing to gain in bringing his name up. Besides, Julia might reach out if she thought I was looking for her without Angus' involvement. A quick glance at the dash clock showed the night was still young. I had hours to roam the streets of Edinburgh and see what I could get out of this. My first port of call decided, I turned off the mobiles and removed the SIM card from both the one I'd been using and the one D. S. Muller had called. If the police were running a location search on my known mobiles, then they wouldn't be able to track me to where I was heading.

First a caffeine fix was required, I would get that on my way. I flipped the gear lever into drive and moved onto the road. Above me, the sky was darkening fast and the wind had begun to tear through the city with a vengeance. Edinburgh was still busy, bad weather or not people still went about their business. I navigated my big Audi through the streets at a leisurely pace, thinking best when I was on the move. A Bruce Springsteen song started on the radio, Murder Incorporated, I couldn't help but grin. Fitting! I drove westward, heading towards Julia Felt's home address. Not that I expected her to be there, but it was a natural place to start looking. I wanted to get inside, look around and see if I could find anything of value. I had the tools and the know-how to break in if the risk was acceptable.

Julia's home lay outside the Edinburgh bypass, in a nice residential area. My sat-nav guided me to a detached house with a garden, in a mature neighbourhood. It was more of a family home than a single-person dwelling. Maybe she liked her privacy and space, or maybe it was bought as an investment. Regardless, it suited me just fine. The house was shielded from the street and the weather kept people indoors, except for the most determined dog owners. I drove up and down the street before I found a secluded parking space a couple of streets away. The house appeared dark as I slowly drove past it, but my view was restricted. I did notice a security alarm box on the front of it and noted the security provider: Castle Rock Security.

I reached for a third mobile, unregistered to my name or business and called Petite on a secure receiving line, which she answered within seconds.

"Hugo, talk to me."

"Everything okay?" I asked quickly.

"Yes, I'm still digging. And, the police detective called again. She wants to talk to you."

"Is it urgent? Did she say why?" I asked.

"Well, she said it's fairly urgent, whatever that means. But she wasn't demanding or anything. Sounded quite cool and calm to me. She wouldn't say why she wanted to talk to you though. Must be related to this Jens fella. Anyway, I've done some light digging on Rachel Muller, interesting it is and pretty dramatic – and I've only just scratched the surface. I'll send you what I've got as soon as I can."

"Great, keep it coming, I need information, I'm being played here and I need to figure this out before it blows up," I said, pausing to look around. The rain was now pounding on the roof of my Audi. There was silence on Petite's side whilst she was thinking about this mess and then just as I would've expected, she got right to the point.

"Are you thinking you might be framed for the killing of this Jens guy?"

"Maybe, but one thing's for sure: I'm being played here, but I'm not sure by whom."

"Right, what's your next move, Hugo?"

"Well. I've tried to get hold of Chris Lafferty, but there's no answer. I don't know who else to trust within the force just now. There is another guy, but I haven't decided yet ... can you reach out and see if you can uncover anything?" Petite had contacts too and she was not such a marked person as me.

"Will do, Hugo. But if you've been framed for this, wouldn't the police be here by now? I've taken precautions for that anyway: your office is clean; the doors are locked and cameras working; a couple of commands to enter on the computer and all our files will disappear into the darkness. If they arrive with a search warrant, I'll shut everything down before letting them in." Petite laughed, her voice sounded triumphant. I had no doubt she got a kick out of this stuff.

"Brilliant." I replied, genuinely pleased, Petite had, without needing to be prompted, turned the office into a fortress. "You staying over? Feel free, the fridge is stocked and there's clean bedding and stuff in the domestic cupboard." I wasn't going home, but it would be ace if she stayed and continued working.

"Yes, I will. I think you need help to save your ass, Hugo – again." Petite was right, I did need her help. Again.

"Sure do, thank you. Listen I'm not coming back, I'm staying away for now. But I need you to do some more online magic for me."

"Name it," Petite replied quickly, eager to help.

"I need you hack the mainframe security computer of Castle Rock Security, locate Julia Felt's home address on the system and disable the alarm. Can you do that?"

It should be possible, particularly for somebody with Petite's skills. I knew a guy within that firm who, after a few too many beers one evening, told me about his frustration regarding a flaw in the system. At the time I didn't make a big deal about it, but I did make a mental note. Now it had come in handy. I heard machine-gun-like typing on Petite's keyboard and waited.

"They have security and firewalls," Petite said, more to herself than me. More typing. I continued to wait. "Decent enough security, but no match for me, Hugo." The tapping on the keyboard continued with lightning speed. "How long do you need, Hugo?"

"Give me until five minutes to midnight."

That should be enough time to get in, look around and get out safely. The system would be back on for what I knew would be a routine midnight automatic check. That was information I'd gained from the loose tongue of the security company's employee who'd been fishing for a job with me, but had talked himself out of any offerings. He thought he'd been clever, moaning on about the shortcomings of his current employer, but I knew I couldn't trust a guy like that.

"Right. It's done. It'll turn itself back on five minutes before midnight and only a comprehensive review will reveal the breach. Call me again, I'll monitor it from here. If there's any activity, I'll let you know. Stay safe."

"Thank you, you are gold."

Outside the clouds had opened and it was pouring down. Combined with the wind, it made for a thoroughly miserable Edinburgh evening, but good for what I was planning to do. I deleted the search history in my sat-nav, took off my leather jacket and pulled a black all-weather coat with a hood from the back seat. In the boot I carried a rucksack with tools that I would need for a job like this. Grabbing that and pair of black gloves I headed off.

The street was deserted and the houses along it all sat back from the street, shielded by walls, bushes and trees. It was a neighbourhood of people with money who liked their privacy. Julia's property had a six-foot stone wall running around it, with a solid metal gate which was shut and, presumably, locked. I sheltered in a dark corner of the edge of the wall and looked around. As far as I could see from where I was standing nobody from the neighbouring houses could see me. Petite had hacked the mainframe of the house security, disabling both the sensor-activated lights and the CCTV, so I just had to get over the wall or through the gate without being seen. Out of my rucksack I took a small but powerful all-weather drone. It had a camera linked to the screen of my hand-held controls. There was also an infrared option, which was just as well as the darkness was so thick it was now sliceable. This was a very expensive piece of kit, but definitely worth it. I flew it up to quickly inspect the top of the wall, and sure enough, embedded in the top were concrete-fixed, sharp metal edges or broken glass. I then flew the drone around the house inspecting it as well as I could do considering the conditions. The house was in darkness, so if Julia was in there she was either sleeping, sitting in the dark, or in a room that didn't give out light. I flew the drone back and quickly packed it away.

I needed to get over that wall, despite its embedded deterrents. The weather was horrible, but there was always the possibility of a nutter dog owner who walked his dog regardless, so I would have to be on the look-out for him. From my rucksack I pulled out a thick, padded mat, which, with the help of a telescopic pole, I laid on top of the wall, then used another telescopic pole to climb up onto it. I carefully rolled over on the mat, trying to avoid the sharp spikes that were poking through just enough to be felt. Still, it was doable. I pulled up the climbing pole and dropped it, together with my rucksack, down on the inside of the wall. Next, I carefully lowered myself into the garden and left the climbing pole up against the wall. I had to leave my mat laid on top as it was embedded on the spikes and wouldn't move.

I stood still for a minute in the garden and just listened. Nothing. Quickly I moved towards a side door of the house. I had decided to make this my entry point. The lock was solid, but breakable. Within a minute it had clicked and the door was open. It was all about the tools, as well as the know-how. I cautiously pushed the door open and waited. No dog came charging, nor did any alarm start. I stepped inside, closing the door behind me. I was standing in a modern, spacious, open-plan dining-kitchen. Julia was a tidy person from what I could see; the inside resembled a show house. Looking around, I quickly changed my mind – this wasn't really a home. It didn't seem to be lived in, there were no dishes in the sink or on the worktops – it appeared that nobody had been here for weeks. There was a slightly strange scent in the air, not pungent, but not pleasant either – chemical in some sense. I started moving through the kitchen, opening drawers and cupboards, looking for something – anything – but I found nothing of interest. I quickly moved through the ground floor. The front door didn't have a letter box, so the mail must be delivered, I assumed, to a box at the gate. The rest of the downstairs was very much like the kitchen-dining room, clean and tidy. Sterile in fact.

I didn't find anything of interest until I focused on the paintings on Julia's walls. There were many of them, more than would be considered to be normal. I noticed they were all covered with see-through film. All of the downstairs walls were covered with paintings of various sizes. It took me a moment before I realised that they all appeared to come from the same art dealer. I moved in close to a large-framed painting in Julia's living room and read with interest a small brass label on the frame: Ariella Cantor Art Studio. I didn't recognise the artist, but that wasn't my field of expertise. I checked the other frames: they all carried Ariella Cantor's label. I noticed that they were all by different artists and all looked ... well, just expensive. I stood back in the middle of the living room and took a moment to consider the implications of the situation. There was something about this that I wasn't able to see right away, but there was definitely something about this that rang alarm bells in me. I stood still and kept looking. I could sense it, it would come to me, it was on the tip of my tongue.

Ariella Cantor was the lady who had approached me six months ago with the case of her missing daughter, Chloe. The little girl had been missing for months, fate unknown. Ariella Cantor was a renowned Edinburgh-based art dealer and, as it turned out, a lady deeply immersed in organised crime. I had taken the case and my life had unravelled from then on. I last spoke to her about a month ago. I hadn't really admitted it to myself, let alone to anyone else, but I found Ariella very attractive.

I surveyed the scene, letting my instinct work through the potential scenarios that were popping up in my head. And then it dawned on me what I was looking at: this wasn't art, this was storage of something very different. Julia was providing a service for Ariella Cantor, but not the art dealer, Ariella Cantor. All right, but was this linked to the game? If so, how? No viable explanation presented itself as I slowly walked around the downstairs, looking and checking.

I went upstairs, but found nothing, Strangely, there wasn't even a shred of evidence to suggest that anybody had been living here for several weeks, if not months. Nothing! No paper work of interest and no hidden safe that I could locate. I stood for a while, listening to the walls, but they were silent. Nothing presented itself as a clue as to where Julia was hiding.

I was just about to go downstairs when I heard the unmistakable sound of a door being unlocked ...

NINE

"Listen guys, we need to remove all the paintings from the ground floor. All the paintings – bring them out to the van. And we need to be fast, really fast."

The man's voice was stressed and urgent as he issued these instructions. I recognised it immediately – it was Jimmy Johnson! The heavy rain had masked the sound of their entry and by the time I realised the front door was being unlocked it was too late. Jimmy had a key.

"Got it Jimmy," another gruff voice replied, then growled, "Right John, let's get going."

John, in turn, spoke a few indecipherable, guttural words.

I had eased myself away from the upstairs landing and was standing very still as I listened to the men downstairs rushing in and out. Controlling my breathing, I coldly considered my options. I wasn't armed, other than with a solid large Maglite, which could be used as a baton if required. Downstairs, the frenzied activity continued. It appeared that in their rush nobody had noticed there was somebody else in the house.

"Come on guys, we need this done."

Unmistakably, that was Jimmy's voice. My good friend Jimmy, who I'd been talking to just a few hours earlier. My lawyer. Well, now I understood why his vibe had spooked me. Jimmy was involved – in what capacity I had yet to discover – but he was involved. I just knew venturing downstairs wouldn't be a good idea. Lifelong friends or not, I couldn't trust Jimmy now, but if I could get out of this predicament without him recognising me, I would have an angle on this. The men downstairs were working so fast and furiously they didn't appear to have detected my break-in or presence. Yet.

A thud resounded through the house and I heard Jimmy curse. It sounded like that one had hit a door frame, or something hard, with one of the picture frames. The guy shot back an angry reply and a heated exchanged followed. For a moment I wondered if they were going to go for each other, and I considered using the commotion to charge downstairs and club them all down. But they all calmed down and got back on with the task at hand. I waited. Jimmy could handle himself, and there were at least two others with him. Besides, so far, I was fine in my hiding position.

"That's it downstairs, Jimmy. You want the frames from upstairs?"

I rolled my shoulders, loosened up and pulled down my ski mask. If they came upstairs, the game was up and I would need to fight my way out. I quickly decided on a plan. Keep it simple. I would charge them as they came up the stairs, using my downward momentum to kick and club them down. A successful fight is rarely won by finesse, it's won by determination and sheer brute force. It's ugly and chaotic, frantic and dirty. The one with the momentum should win. It was me against a minimum of three, so I needed to have momentum on my side.

"Jimmy? You listening?" The voice sounded urgent. I waited for a response. Why didn't Jimmy answer? Had he discovered the presence of somebody else in the house? The noise of people moving downstairs continued.

"Jimmy?" The gruff voice was now closer, moving in my direction. I got ready to take the guy out whilst he was moving up the stairs and then charge past him.

"John, what are you doing, man?"

"Going upstairs Jimmy..."

"No, there's nothing up there. We got to move – now!"

"Okay, whatever."

The guy on the stairs went down, and within a couple of minutes the front door was shut and what sounded like a van drove away. I waited. This had been a close call, but it wasn't over yet. Jimmy and his crew could still be out there. The heavy rain continued lashing down with a vengeance. I waited, five minutes, ten minutes, just listening. Then it was time for me to move. I went to the front bedroom and peeked through the vertical blind. The room was dark, but my vision had adjusted so I could navigate the space without bumping into stuff. Outside there was no van and the gate seemed to be closed. They had definitely left. Questions raced through my head as I struggled to digest the latest dramatic development. What was that all about? Who was Jimmy working for?

I went downstairs and had a quick look around. All the paintings were gone. The guys had certainly been in a hurry, some of the furniture had been overturned. I left the house the way I'd entered, through the kitchen door. The rain was even heavier than earlier. Perfect. I took a moment to scan the surroundings and saw nothing to cause alarm. Then I ran across to where my telescopic climbing pole stood, but hearing a car coming up the street I waited before starting to climb. The entrance gate to my left swung open and a big black saloon car drove through. I stood very still and leaned against the climbing pole, trying to blend in with the wall. The rain and darkness made it impossible to see who was in the car, and I hoped the same elements were working in my favour too, concealing my presence. The car drove up to the house, so I decided to go for it; I charged up the wall, dropped my rucksack down on the other side and rolled over.

"Hey you ...," a voice shouted through the rain.

But I was already over the wall, I grabbed my rucksack and ran down the street. I heard the car engine firing up. I knew it was coming, but it was pointing in the wrong direction. The driver would either have to turn, or reverse out, both of which would give me a couple of minutes' advantage. I just needed to get to the end of the street and turn the corner before the car came back on the road. I was sure the gate had been closed, another few seconds in my favour. I made it around the corner and calculated I had less than a minute to clear the next one. I ran as fast as I could. Again, I made it. Both sides of the street had trees lining the pavement. I slid behind a big tree and listened. I thought I could hear a car, but it didn't appear. Minutes passed. The tree shielded me from the worst of the rain. I wanted to get back to my car and get away, but my instinct told me to wait. Just as well, as a couple of minutes later the car came around the corner at speed. It passed my position and stopped abruptly at the end of the street. For a long moment it just remained there, its powerful engine snarling restlessly. It was a big Mercedes, a saloon car, performance model, not the type the police would drive, but something gangsters would. Were they Ariella Cantor's men, or another crew? I'd spotted two guys in front, a driver and a guy riding shotgun, but my view was so fleeting I couldn't see who it was. I carefully slid further around the tree, putting the thick trunk between myself and the car. It stood there, idling. They had lost me, and I presumed they must now be discussing what to do next, possibly checking with the boss. I could just make out the number plate, which I memorised. Then the car took off with spinning tyres, disappearing around the corner.

I waited another minute and then headed back. The rain had penetrated my clothing and I was wet and miserable. I decided to find a hotel room and take stock. But first, I made a quick phone call to Tam, who assured me that Claire and Emily were being watched and were safe.

Just over two hours later I opened the door to the bland, but totally adequate, hotel room just outside Stirling, central Scotland. I had headed west, leaving Edinburgh behind for now. Driving up the M9, I decided on the hotel as I approached the Stirling motorway services. I needed some space and distance from Edinburgh, hopefully to get some perspective and figure out my next moves. A sleepy receptionist took my reservation booking, made from the car park immediately before entering the hotel. He hardly looked at me, gave me the room key card, mumbled something about breakfast, tried to stifle a mighty yawn and then excused himself. I waited until he'd disappeared before I headed off to my room. I felt stiff and tired. But then again it had been a very eventful day. A steaming hot shower was required before bed. But there were things I still needed to do. I hadn't called Petite yet. My mind had been preoccupied with Jimmy, and I had even had doubts about Petite! Was she involved? I thought back to the look I'd seen between Petite and Jimmy earlier today; had it been meaningful, or had I imagined that? It's easy to make connections that don't actually exist when doubt has the upper hand.

If I couldn't trust Petite, then I was in real trouble. She was the one who had my back. I paced the hotel room in nothing but my boxer shorts, cursing under my breath. Damn! What a mess. I took out my phone and made a decision: I would continue to trust Petite. Time would tell if that was a mistake. I turned it on and waited as the screen came to life. Four missed calls and a couple of texts, all from Petite. She was wondering what was going on. They all appeared genuine. I swiped the screen and called her. She answered immediately.

"Hugo, finally!"

"Yes, just to let you know, I'm fine. How're things at your end?"

"Well, the police haven't turned up yet, but I've got some interesting findings from my digging. You need to know this ..." Petite's voice was calm and neutral, the way she spoke when the heat was on.

"I'm all ears," I said as I stared out of the window.

"Okay, it's about Jimmy – he's involved ..." Her voice trailed off.

"I know," I replied quickly, grabbing the opportunity to speak.

"What – what do you know?" Petite sounded stunned.

"I was at Julia's house when he turned up with a crew and cleared the house of a bunch of paintings, in a big hurry. I don't know any more than that. Now, your turn," I said, and waited.

A little silence elapsed, then Petite replied, "Well, it's not only this Jens Brekken making a substantial payment to Julia, it's Julia making the same payment to Jimmy a couple of days later – the exact same amount as Jens had paid to her. But what on earth was Jimmy doing picking up paintings at Julia's house this evening? What sort of paintings are we talking about here anyway?"

"Art – all paintings from Ariella Cantor's Studio in Edinburgh. I was there, Petite, upstairs as he and a couple of other guys cleared out the downstairs."

"You're joking. Ariella Cantor? That's a ghost from the not-too-distant past. They didn't notice you then?" Petite continued to sound stunned and I felt a little guilty for having doubted her, but I put that aside.

"You need to expand your digging – Ariella Cantor next. Got anything on that Detective Sergeant Muller yet?"

The words were hardly out of my mouth when I noticed a big, black Mercedes saloon pulling into the combined service station and hotel car park beneath my window. Stepping back from the window, I quickly turned off the lights in my room. Petite realised that something was going on.

"You okay there, Hugo?"

I was back at the window, now with the curtains almost closed over. I had a view of the car, but I couldn't see its number plates. However, it was like the one that had pulled up at Julia's house earlier. The longer I looked at it, the more certain I became that it was the same car. Nobody got out. How on earth had they traced me? I'd been certain nobody had followed me up the M9. I looked over at my car; it was parked in full view of the big Mercedes. A thought hit me.

"Listen, Petite, can you run a plate for me?"

I knew Petite had experience of hacking the DVLA, Driver Vehicle Licensing Agency, it was a handy tool for our business. My urgency was obvious and Petite was switched on, so she didn't waste time asking questions. I heard machine-gun-fast typing before she came back on.

"What's the number plate?"

I trotted out the details from memory as I kept looking at the big Mercedes. I knew it was the same car, and the guys inside were waiting. A few minutes passed as Petite ran the number. Then I heard a slight gasp. Petite gathered her composure and came back.

"It's registered to Kenny Bullard."

TEN

Kenny Bullard was Cameron Bullard's oldest son, who for almost a decade had been the heir apparent of the criminal empire currently run by his father. He was an unpleasant type, violent, vindictive and mean, lacking all the nicer features that made his dad seem somewhat human. Kenny and I didn't get along, we never had, and I knew the son was itching to finish me off. But he'd been in Spain for the last two years, and I'd almost forgotten about him.

Kenny was the gangster version of the frustrated, inheritance kid – disappointed to still be waiting for what I knew he considered to be his rightful place: at the very top, the one in charge. But his father didn't want to retire, and he just kept on living. Maybe Cameron, knew, deep down, that Kenny was a bad apple, rotten to the core, and if he took over, it would be the beginning of the end for the Bullard criminal enterprise. These were all philosophical issues that I didn't have time, nor inclination, to consider right now.

Petite knew this as well. She knew about Kenny, not in depth, but enough. Before Kenny's forced relocation to Spain, he'd tried to chat her up, but got a firm no. Kenny wasn't the type to accept a 'no' from a female, but Petite had more clout than most other young women and Kenny backed off. Petite did it with her usual finesse, even though I knew she couldn't stand the man. Not many could, but he was Cameron's chosen successor, thus one kept negative opinions to oneself. Kenny was the type who took everything personally, just like a child and he would lash out spontaneously, without any thought about consequences. He used to be like that anyway – maybe, he'd changed? For the last couple of years he'd been exiled to Spain, so to speak, cooling down after an incident that his dad had been forced to sort. Maybe, he'd grown up? If they were his guys out there, then he would definitely be capable enough of tracking me down.

"Where are you anyway?" Petite asked.

I was still at the window, having quickly got dressed in the darkness of my room. There would be no hot shower, nor any sleep – not here anyway. The Mercedes was still parked down below, but nobody had left the car yet. I could see light inside the cabin, but not much else.

"In a hotel at the main M9 services outside Stirling," I replied as I glanced over at my car.

"How did they follow you up there?" Petite gasped again, as it dawned on her what I had already realised a little earlier. "Your car ... they got somebody clever to hack your car sat-nav. I meant to speak to you about that, guess its too late now ..." Petite cursed under her breath. She was angry with herself, livid in fact. I could sense her intense fury.

Yep, too late, I thought to myself. It had likewise occurred to me that I was vulnerable in that regard, but I'd never got around to dealing with it. A sloppy, careless mistake, but it was my mistake. My car, a high-tech machine, with a mobile computer online, was hackable through its connections to the world around it!

"Listen, don't beat yourself up, Petite. I should've done something about it myself, it's my flamin' car. There might be a tracker on it. Anyway, I've got to deal with this, here and now."

"What's happening, Hugo?"

"Nothing, they're just waiting in their car."

"Why?"

"Guess they're waiting for back up," I suggested. I wanted to see who was in the car.

Petite knew better than to give me lame advice, so sticking with the facts, she said, "Hugo, there're a couple of things you need to know."

"Okay," I replied calmly.

"I got this email, just under an hour ago – it came to the business address, for your attention. It says: 'Hugo, remember: tick, tock, tick, tock, remember Wide Open Eyes.'" Petite stopped, it was a stupid message that we would normally laugh off, but we didn't now.

My jaw tightened. So, Father Black thought he was funny? I didn't need this silliness, but I guess it gave him a kick doing it. "Who's the sender?" I asked just for confirmation. Petite didn't answer right away. I knew it wasn't straightforward. Nothing was. "Come on, Petite, tell me, who's the sender?"

"Well, this doesn't make sense, but it was sent from the Law firm of Johnson and Associates."

I clenched my fists – the email had come from Jimmy's firm. "You're right, Petite, this doesn't make sense. You're the tech geek here, but I guess somebody could've used Jimmy's email to send this message?"

"Sure, not that difficult really, but if it's Father Black, then he certainly has upped his game."

"Possibly, but I'm thinking Kenny, as he's proved he has the expertise available – yeah, I think this is Kenny. It looks like the Bullard crew has entered the twenty-first century... " I paused as I saw the Mercedes doors open; two big guys dressed in black stepped out. "Hold on ..." I said, turning my attention to the two guys. They both looked up and I saw their faces. I didn't recognise the driver, but the front seat passenger, I did. It was possible they could've seen my shape in the window, but I knew they couldn't have identified me; I was in the dark, they were in the light of the outdoors. They glanced at each other, the driver looked back at the entrance of the car park and nodded to the bigger guy. Then they moved forward and disappeared from my view. They were coming in. I felt the first hit of adrenaline surging through my veins.

Come and get me, Mike Cunningham! I whispered to myself as I quickly got my stuff together. I was on the second floor, the top floor of the box that was this hotel. The layout was standard: a central corridor running across with rooms on each side, stairs either end with another staircase and a lift in the middle. My habit of quickly memorising the layout of any building I was in, meant I had options. I could make my escape or wait. There were two of them just now, but there would be more.

I remained at the window as another two black Mercedes saloon cars drove quickly into the car park and came to a halt in front of the hotel. Six guys piled out and also disappeared from my view. Eight in total. It was time to go.

"Petite, I need a different car. I'll call you back," I said, terminating the call as I stepped into the corridor. I'd disabled the lift earlier, by blocking the door from shutting, but I now removed the block and immediately the lift started to go down – someone had pressed the call button. This would make at least a couple of them stand there waiting for it to arrive, leaving two on each staircase coming up. The eight of them would be tied up for the next few minutes, allowing me to get out by the fire-escape rope at the back of the hotel, just off a domestic storage room. I ran there, hit the fire alarm, opened the window, threw out the rope and climbed out. It was dark behind the hotel as it was shaded by a small woodland of some sort. I slid down the rope, which I'd covered in an alcoholic cleaning fluid taken from the domestic room. Even though I was wearing gloves, my hands started to burn during my descent, but I ignored the pain. Inside the hotel the alarm was sounding, and a few lights were coming on. On the ground I removed what was left of my gloves and took care as I lit the rope. Unavoidably, some of the liquid had got on my hair and clothes, but I managed to light the rope without torching myself. The flames hungrily ate into it, rendering it useless for anybody else, but I was sure the hotel itself shouldn't burn. The alarm was sounding loudly, waking up the few guests inside and notifying the fire service. It was also complicating things for Mike and his crew. I disappeared into the woods and started to run. Even though

I had the vile taste of the cleaning fluid on my tongue, I couldn't help but laugh. It felt good to feel the adrenaline pumping through my body.

I wasn't followed; the fire alarm and my swift escape saw to that. Fighting through the small woodland at the back of the hotel, I got soaked. It wasn't raining, but it had been, and both the ground and vegetation were wet. The service station was strategically positioned for access to the M9 between Stirling and Edinburgh, and the M8 heading towards Glasgow. I arrived at a big roundabout and quickly crossed the exit roads, onto the A782 heading towards a place called Denny. I started walking in that direction, feeling rather exposed, but unable to think of a better plan. It was just past one in the morning and fatigue was overtaking me, but I pressed on. My Audi was out of commission for the time being and I needed a replacement. Hopefully Petite had taken care of that. I got out my phone and rang her.

"Talk to me Hugo."

"I got away. I need that car, Petite. Is it sorted?"

"Yes, Steve's coming for you, where are you?"

"Steve? Who's he?"

"One of my cousins, he lives in Stirling. He's totally dependable, didn't even hesitate when I called and woke him up. He's heading your way as we speak. You can have the car, just drop him back in Stirling. That's okay, isn't it?"

"Yes, of course, and thank you." If Petite trusted him, so would I. Looking around, I continued, "I'm heading towards Denny, on the A872. I'm pretty exposed here, Petite...," my voice trailed off as I heard an engine approaching and threw myself down in a ditch beside the road. Its headlights swiped over where I'd just been walking, but the car drove past at speed. I looked up in time to see the rear lights of a Mercedes disappearing around the bend ahead. I couldn't tell for sure if it was one of the Bullard cars, but my gut told me it was. They hadn't given up yet.

"Hugo, what happened?" Petite's intense voice got my attention. I didn't get up, just lay there, ignoring the cold, and watching the road. No other cars came, but it had been a close call. So far, I'd been lucky, but luck only ran so far.

"They're still looking for me. When can Steve be here?" I got up. My clothes wet and caked in dirt and mud. I hoped this Steve fella wasn't too bothered about his car interior.

"In ten minutes, I think. Hold on, I'll check." I heard Petite talking on a different phone. "Make that five minutes, Hugo, you stand ready to jump in."

"You got it, what's he driving?" I started walking back the way.

"A Vauxhall Insignia VRX estate, it's blue. And very fast."

"Great. let me focus on this just now. I'll call you back." I was certain I could tell the difference between the headlights of a Mercedes and a Vauxhall. Just under four minutes now.

"You got it, Hugo. Call me though, as soon as you can." With that, Petite terminated the call, and I quickly dialled again. The number rang a few times before a clear voice answered.

"Tam speaking."

"Hi Tam, it's Hugo. Just a quick call – Claire and Emily still okay? Everything fine?" I tried to sound casual, but I could feel the clammy hand of panic grabbing my spine.

"Yes, they're sleeping, presumably. Nothing happening here, Hugo. What's going on with you?" Tam's voice was on the alert.

I looked around before answering, "I'm being hunted, Tam, this is turning crazy. I don't know what's going on." My voice carried an intensity that Tam recognised; he'd been in many a sticky situation before.

"Got it partner, I'll make sure Claire and Emily are safe."

"Thanks. I'll get back to you," I said, ending the call.

I walked on and looked at my watch. Just under two minutes now. Another engine roared in the distance, causing me to stop. Judging by the high-pitched snarl, it was a performance engine. The Insignia VRX has a 2.8 V6 turbo, a rather small engine when compared to the big blocks offered by the Germans. Then I heard yet another roar, this too was a performance petrol engine and more like a big German. It was coming from the other direction, the direction the Mercedes had been going. I stepped back from the road. There wasn't much time. Then a set of headlights appeared, cutting through the darkness. I made my decision.

ELEVEN

"Hold on!" Steve shouted, as he floored the accelerator. The turbo up front kicked in, the engine screamed, and the heavy wagon leaped forward. I did as instructed, whilst looking in the rear-view mirror at the Mercedes in hot pursuit behind us; it had the power to stay close on our tails. We were fast approaching the service station roundabout, but Steve didn't seem to be easing off the gas. I glanced over at the man and saw the determination in his tight jaw – he wasn't about to slow down. I said a silent prayer that there wouldn't be any traffic on the roundabout. The chassis screamed its complaint as we hit the roundabout at the limit of its capacity.

"Look out!" I shouted instinctively as I saw a BMW X5 police car roll out in front of us from the service station exit. It came to an abrupt halt, its blue lights flashing.

"Got it," Steve shouted back. His responsiveness at the wheel was awesome. The startled faces of the police officers were visible for a fleeting second as we shot past their front bumper. The wagon fish-tailed, and I wondered if this was it. Steve worked the wheel instinctively and got the car back under control. The driver of the Mercedes behind us wasn't as quick though and rammed the police car with an almighty bang. A few seconds later we were off the roundabout heading down the country road towards Bannockburn. Sirens were going crazy behind us. Steve eased off the speed and we drove on, just a little over the speed limit. I could feel the pulse throbbing in my jugular vein. A set of flashing lights appeared from the bend in front of us, bathing the colourless darkness around us in a cold blue light.

"Damn." Steve said through gritted teeth.

I reached out, laid a hand on his shoulder and said, "Keep it cool mate – just drive on. There's nothing but chaos at that scene right now."

I focused on the approaching vehicle with the flashing blue lights: it was an ambulance. Steve grunted a reply and drove on as the vehicle shot past us, sirens screeching, while the medics inside focused on the job ahead. I wondered if there were any fatalities at the scene? The Mercedes had rammed the police car at high speed, so that was a distinct possibility. I looked over at Steve and saw the worry in his face; he was probably thinking the same as me. He surely couldn't have anticipated any of this when he'd said yes to Petite's plea just under an hour ago. Not sure what to say next, I stared out of the window. Regardless, there would be consequences, and if any police officers had been killed, the heat would be unbearable. This was yet another unwanted complication to deal with.

I sensed Steve anxiously glancing over at me and I turned to face him. Our eyes met for a second before he focused back on the road, but I kept looking at him. The worry in his eyes had been replaced by fury.

"Listen Steve, I'm really grateful for this. Thank you." All my effort was going into producing a calm voice. Steve nodded, but his anger was still obvious.

"I hear you, Hugo Storm. Tell Petite, she now owes me big time. And so do you. The car's yours; it's not registered to me, but to another fella who's currently in Australia – so you owe him too. It's got tax, insurance and a valid MOT. Use it, then get rid of it, but don't bring it back to me – or here! It will be reported stolen in a couple of days. So get rid. You got that, Mr Storm?"

I took a moment, before nodding my agreement. I didn't like his tone, but fair enough, in his shoes I'd have been raging too. "Yeah, I got it," I said, focusing back on the road.

We drove in silence for the next ten minutes until we arrived at Kings Park, Stirling, where Steve pulled into the kerb. He put the car in neutral, letting the engine idle as he checked the immediate surroundings.

"I'm off – remember what I told you."

I offered him my hand. He hesitated for a moment, then with a firm, but moist grip, he shook mine. I understood – this could've gone south. We'd been lucky, no doubt about that.

"Petite should've listened to my uncle," he said, flashing a gritty grin.

"Petite does her own thing, always has, always will," I replied.

Steve got out of the car and proceeded to roll off a set of films from the front and rear number plates, which he tucked into a nearby bin. I looked at him – that was smart. The films of dirt made the number plates impossible to read accurately. The police would possibly have a description of this vehicle, but that was unavoidable. However, thanks to Steve's forethought, they wouldn't have its registration number.

It had turned into a pleasant night, with the promise of a fine morning ahead. The world was sleeping, except for those, like me, roaming the darkness. My clothes were still wet and dirty, and I desperately needed a sleep; my body was aching and my eyelids had started to become heavy. My needs were basic: a shower, a power sleep and a new set of clothes, then I'd be ready to go again. But I knew that was unlikely to happen, so just a little shut eye would do.

"Remember I wasn't here."

I slotted myself behind the wheel, saying, "No worries, mate. And thank you again." I swung the door shut.

Steve looked around for the last time before leaving. As I watched him walk away, I made a mental note to arrange with Petite to transfer him money; after all, he'd just saved me – it was only fair. Regaining my focus, I reached for my phone and made a call. It rang for a long time before Petite's agitated voice answered. She'd been awake for as long as I had, but if she was tired, she didn't show it. A thrill-seeker by nature, she could motor on adrenaline, just like me. But this time I knew something was up.

"Hugo, where are you now?"

"I'm safe, in the car. Our friend has left. There was some drama. What's going on?" I asked.

"The police are coming. I got a tip, Hugo – I've only got minutes, we need to make this quick."

I assumed the police now knew I'd been at the hotel – I'd booked in under my real name as I didn't want to blow either of my two fake identities. These are expensive to obtain if done properly, with the ability to travel internationally included. Anyway, my car was still there in the car park.

"Who gave you the tip?" I asked.

"Chris Lafferty – he's tried to contact you, but he doesn't have the number you're now using. I didn't give it to him either. Figure just now we need to circle the wagons and find out who to trust." More frantic typing from Petite, then, "I'm shutting everything down, Hugo, and sending all your files to the black hole. The police won't find anything," she paused, "I was about to ask if I should contact your lawyer, but that would be Jimmy! What do you want me to do, Hugo?"

I thought hard for a moment before I replied, "No, don't contact Jimmy, just let the police in and answer their questions as best you can. You haven't done anything wrong, so stick to that. Tell them you haven't heard from me since yesterday afternoon. Tell them you're going home to bed."

I stopped as I fought to get a handle on this. Petite was smart and could hold her own. I was as sure I could be that she wouldn't say anything that might close the net on me. But I wanted her to remain at large and not be stuck in a police station.

"Not sure they're gonna buy that, Hugo."

"No, neither am I, but you play it as well as you can. I need to sleep, Petite – I'm shattered. I'll get back to you later."

"All right, Hugo. Hopefully, I won't be in the slammer. I think I'll call my cousin, Jack. He's a lawyer."

Unable to contain it, I yawned; I was so tired. The adrenaline had ebbed away and the tiredness was hitting me like a sledgehammer. It was hard to think straight. I blinked and sat up straight, trying to be alert.

"Yes, do what you've got to do, Petite. I trust you," I replied. I couldn't tell her not to call her cousin, Jack, the lawyer, after all, her cousin Steve had just saved me. Her 'cousin pool' was apparently of high standard.

"Right, speak to you later."

I dropped the phone and drove off. I needed some distance between me and the drama behind; Stirling was too close. It was the early hours of the morning, and an alert could've gone out to all chain motels and hotels. Turning up at a motel looking like I did would probably trigger a discreet phone call to the police if an alert hadn't already been issued. I glanced in the rear-view mirror and decided I would sleep in the car instead. But first I needed to clean up. In my bag I had a spare set of clothes, a bottle of body and hair wash and a towel. I drove on until I found a secluded spot by the river, then got out and looked around: there was nobody to be seen. I needed that situation to continue for the next few minutes. Looking at the dark river made my skin produce goose bumps. For sure, this would be cold! But don't think about it, just do it, I told myself. I stripped, ran down to the river and jumped in. It was cold alright – very cold indeed! I immersed and quickly washed myself, fighting the current from dragging me down the river. A few minutes were enough and I soon ran back up onto land, shivering with cold and feeling like a lunatic, unable to stop laughing. If anybody came upon me now, they would be traumatised for life. I dried myself properly and got dressed. Then I sat in the car and turned the heating on full blast; slowly my body temperature returned to normal. I was clean and dry, and starting to feel better. Looking around, I decided to camp here and have a sleep. I lowered the front windows just a little on both sides, locked the car doors, turned the engine off and reclined my seat. It wasn't the most comfortable sleeping position, but it was good enough, and within a minute the enticing darkness had engulfed me.

TWELVE

A knock awoke me, followed by several others in rapid succession, as I tried to focus and blink the sleep out of my eyes.

"You okay there, Mister?" a voice asked. I looked through the side window of my car, as I raised the back of my seat. An older gentleman was peering in through the window looking at me with a worried expression. I broke a smile, started the engine and lowered the window. The fella stepped back.

"Oh, I'm fine, thank you. I'm on way home to Aberdeen – just needed a sleep. Been down to Southampton for business."

I figured giving the older gentleman a rationale might evaporate any suspicions before they could take hold. The guy looked at me for a moment before deciding to believe me. He was about to say something when a dog barked. A light brown Labrador looked up at me with its dark eyes and the guy started to fuss the dog, providing me with the perfect opportunity to make my escape.

"Well, you have a great day. Sorry – in a hurry to get home to my wife and kids," I said with a wide grin, as I started to ease slowly away. The dog occupied the man enough for me to just drive off. I made sure not to roll over either his feet or the dog's paws as I hit the road. Checking the time, I saw that it was six thirty in the morning, so I'd had a few hours' sleep: enough to keep me going for another day. The clock was ticking, and I still had no idea where Julia was. I needed to get back to Edinburgh and continue my search. The car radio got my attention, so I turned up the volume: news bulletins full of excited presenters talking about the drama at the Stirling M9 services. They said that two police officers had been injured, one was in a critical state, and a civilian had been killed, with another seriously injured in a car crash following a dramatic incident at the services motel. I swallowed hard. My grip on the wheel tightened. This was bad, the police would come after me with a vengeance. I would do well if I managed to stay out of their grasp for the next twenty-four hours. I decided not to head back to Edinburgh the same way as I'd come. The M9 would be a hotspot for police activity. Instead I decided to go west, drive into the Trossachs, and then head south, past Glasgow, cutting east towards Edinburgh through the Scottish Borders region. It meant a drive of several hours on rural roads, but that couldn't be helped. A quick glance at the fuel gauge showed half a tank, so enough to get into calmer waters before I needed to top up.

My phone buzzed – I checked the traffic around me before venturing a quick glance – there were text messages: one from Petite, another from Claire, Emily's mum. My heart rate hiked up a notch; I needed to read both, so I found a lay-by in which to park. The text from Petite was brief and to the point: 'D. S. Muller needs you to contact her immediately on this number ...' I swiped it away, took a gulp of air and opened Claire's text. I could sense her anger in every exclamation mark: 'Hugo, the police are looking for you! This is serious. Contact Detective Sergeant Muller on this number ...! What are you doing?!'

I sat for a while looking at the text, feeling paralysed. I could kiss goodbye access to Emily for the foreseeable future; Claire would fight me tooth and nail, and now she had even more ammo. I couldn't blame her either. If she was angry before, she was furious now. I thumped the steering wheel and cursed; the anger of frustration burned inside me. My world had yet again caused another obstacle to my being with those whom I treasured the most. But did I? Did I in fact treasure my kids the way I professed to? I shook my head, trying to rid myself of those existential thoughts. Too heavy for now. I loved my kids. That wasn't a delusion, and I wouldn't give up – not now, not ever. I would repair the bond with Emily; and I would be there for the three little ones too – somehow.

I drove on, carefully keeping within the speed limits, hoping the cops weren't actively looking for this car – at least not yet. The driving time presented an opportunity to take stock. The last 20 hours or so had been totally chaotic. Father Angus Black had dropped me in at the deep end of a very dangerous game. I took a moment to glance at the beautiful, lush countryside of rural Scotland all around me before focusing back on the road and the plan that was starting to form in my head. I would return to Edinburgh, but wouldn't contact the police, even if that meant a formal warrant would be issued. Sitting in a police station, being questioned about things I had no answers to, including the murder of Jens Brekken, would only be damaging to me. I needed to be proactive, not reactive and completely dependent on external circumstances.

The drive took just over five hours and proceeded without any drama, other than the one I listened to on the radio! Regular news bulletins kept me up-to-date with the situations in Edinburgh and Stirling. Jens Brekken's murder was major news in both the United Kingdom and Norway, and it was spreading even further afield. I guess the narrative of the handsome, poker-playing playboy, executed in a luxury black limousine in an Edinburgh back alley, was just too good to miss.

The Stirling services drama came a strong second in news appeal. I got a jolt at the mention of a certain feared gangster in a national news bulletin. It had been leaked that the infamous Bullard crime family were involved, in an unknown capacity, in this drama. This revelation was now burning its way through the news outlets with the intensity of a fire stoked by aviation fuel. The velocity of my blood, as it raced through my veins, intensified dramatically as I listened to this report. Cameron Bullard would hear about this, and I knew he would immediately begin circling the wagons, so to speak. I also knew he'd issue orders to tie up any loose ends and dispose of problematic matters without delay. That would include me; I was now a marked man. He would have me killed.

The certainty that I was now playing the ultimate game of pure survival only made my focus clearer. In some strange way I felt a certain relief; for months now, I'd been fighting an urge to constantly look back over my shoulder. Every now and again I'd asked myself whether someone could be waiting on the other side of the door, or around the corner. At times, even the most mundane appointments had suddenly become very tense. Umpteen times, I had awoken in the early hours, drenched in sweat, wondering if today was the day when I would be hit by that bullet carrying my name. Because, I was certain that it would come, I just didn't know when and where! At some point, Cameron Bullard would decide that Hugo Storm had been involved in the murder of his missing nephew. At some point, the whispers would be too strong for him to ignore, and the strange affinity he seemed to have for me would finally vanish. The wait now seemed to be over, and that felt oddly liberating. Once and for all, I would have to deal with Cameron Bullard. No more games, no more tripping around the blatantly obvious. Now he would – perhaps with a heavy heart – sanction what so many around him wanted, most of all his oldest son, who was back and ready to assert his position: Hugo Storm must die.

I drove into Edinburgh feeling more invigorated and focused than in a long time. A death sentence tends to sharpen one's mind.

THIRTEEN

If you're trying to find somebody who's in hiding, your best bet is to uncover their link to the outside world, then narrow down the pool of candidates to a minimum and hit them smart before they have time to disappear.

With that principle in mind, Julia didn't have any family; the ones she shared a blood link with were deplorable – she wouldn't want to be associated with any of them. Julia had created her own world of friends and family as she'd fought herself out of the mayhem that had characterised her childhood. I knew a few candidates in her pool. I'd already reached out to Sheila. With my game plan for the day I left the car in a Park and Ride just inside the Edinburgh bypass, up from Little France, and jumped on a bus heading into the city centre.

I stared out the bus window – it was a fine day for a change: blue sky and sun. Yesterday it had poured down with a vengeance, but today was beautiful. Typical Edinburgh – and Scotland as a whole, for that matter. I loved this place. I'd decided to ignore everything else, the police, the Bullards, Jimmy, even Claire and Emily; Tam had my back on those two. Today, I would trawl through Edinburgh, leaving no stone unturned, until I found Julia. I was determined to do so, one way or another.

The bus passed Edinburgh Royal Infirmary and continued its slow journey towards the centre. People got on and off; nobody paid any attention to me. A free Metro newspaper lay on the empty seat in front of me, so I picked it up. The headline announced the discovery of Jens Brekken's body. Not much more detail followed in the article itself, but then again I assumed the story had been written in a hurry to meet the print deadline. I learned nothing new, so put the paper down. The bus had reached the city centre, where the majestic old stone buildings of Edinburgh stood proudly on both sides of the street. It was busy with people everywhere. Edinburgh was always busy: 'alive 365, with a pulse and a vibe'. That translated into energy for me.

I got off the bus near the Royal Mile and headed for my first port of call. I had called Sir Ian Keller's secretary earlier to cancel our nine o'clock meeting, and had snatched a quick word with the man himself. He just told me to pop by later, whenever I could. I was very thankful for that, as I knew Ian to be an extremely busy man, something his fiercely-protective personal secretary had managed to tell me twice as she grudgingly put me through. Ian knew Julia, being one of her well-established clients. A risk-taker by nature, he had regularly fronted the money for Julia's poker games. He did it for the buzz, and I knew that. During the long drive to Edinburgh I'd had time to think, and I figured that if Sheila couldn't produce a result, maybe Ian could help me.

Sir Ian's HQ was in the city centre. He had resisted the temptation to relocate to one of the business parks on the outskirts. The man was all about the tech, but funnily enough, he didn't like the idea of being in a glass tower, stuck in a field outside the city. He had also resisted relocating to London, New York or any other global city. I guess he considered the world was a village and all that jazz. I arrived at the heavy wooden door of his HQ building. It was a beautiful stone building from the early 1900s, but in this part of Edinburgh, that was rather modern. I rang the bell and a smooth, energetic voice answered through the intercom. I identified myself, and was buzzed in. Inside it was modern, hip and beautiful: a tasteful blend of solid wood, gleaming stone and brushed steel. The stairs up to Reception were made of reinforced glass in shades of blue and green. They looked to me like the sea around a Caribbean island. Reception itself was just as beautiful, as was the drop-dead-gorgeous receptionist who greeted me. She flashed a set of perfect, sparkling-white teeth and informed me that Sir

Ian Keller was ready to see me straight away. She was truly beautiful. I'd be willing to bet that she spoke at least four languages and had a brain that could quadruple-task.

Taking the stairs up to the executive floor, I passed a few more people, all of whom were beautiful or handsome, smartly dressed and pulsing the vibe of success. I had arrived, so it seemed, in the world of beautiful, successful people.

Ian was at the window, sipping a cup of coffee when I entered his office. The guy was just in his early forties and liked to look good. He was wearing dark, pinstriped suit trousers and a white silk shirt with bright red suspenders. A pair of vibrant, yellow-framed glasses and dark brown hair framed a ruggedly-handsome, tanned face. Ian liked to exercise in the fresh air; mountain sports were some of his passions, in keeping with his character. He turned to smile and greet me as I entered.

"Ah, Hugo, come in. Have a coffee – it's perfect: a new Columbian brand. Its lush! I might invest. A couple of young lads in Leith have taken it upon themselves to make Scotland a better place by importing this wonderful coffee."

I accepted his invitation to pour myself a cuppa. The aroma was inviting. I lifted the cup in a toast-like gesture to Ian and took a sip: he was right, it was truly perfect. He leaned against his desk, smiling as he awaited my verdict.

"Yep, that's lush."

Ian seemed satisfied at that and gestured for me to have a seat, but he remained standing. I sat down and placed my cup on a small coffee table between the two leather chairs in front of his huge desk. We looked at each other, the pleasantries over, it was now time to get down to business.

"So, what's going on?" Ian's smile had gone.

I looked back at him for a moment and decided to continue with my plan. "A lot, Ian. It's complicated. The bottom line is that I need to reach Julia Felt – her life is in danger." I paused for effect, my voice had conveyed the urgency I genuinely felt.

Ian didn't reply, but just looked at me before he pushed off from his desk, walked around it and sat down. Leaning his elbows on the desk, he folded his hands together and linked his fingers, except for his index ones, which he pointed at me.

"You don't waste time, do you, Hugo. I've seen the breaking news – are you involved in this?"

"Not by choice, Ian. I'm being framed here. I've got to find Julia," I replied emphatically.

Ian nodded slightly, probably without thinking, and I knew he was intrigued. The guy was an instinctive risk-taker, an adrenaline-junkie. He preferred action to words; the way he conducted himself in his business proved that. Luckily for him, his instinct was mostly right, which meant the money pile kept growing bigger.

"This is deadly serious, Ian. This dead Norwegian is part of this, and there's more, much more – I don't know exactly what Julia's involvement is, hiding isn't an option though. If I can't go to her, then she needs to come to me."

I paused and attempted to get a reading from his body language: nothing – just his sharp, thoughtful eyes studying me. He was evaluating my sincerity, no doubt, and I was reminded of how this guy had become wealthy: he wasn't just a risk-taker, he was also smart, very smart.

"I understand, but I can't help you on this, Hugo. I don't know where she is either."

Ian kept his eyes on me. The easy smile had gone, he was now totally stone-faced. I leaned back, taking a moment to consider if I should try to press on. I decided not to; applying pressure would only be counter-productive.

Clearing his throat, Ian continued, "Right, Hugo, I wanted to see you here today because I've got a job for you – but considering what's going on, it can wait ...," Ian took another sip of his coffee. He looked at me intensely for a moment before he continued, "I know what you're thinking, Hugo."

"What would that be?" My tone was respectful as I asked the question he'd primed me for.

"That I'm lying, and know where she is – I don't, but since I like you, Hugo, I'll give you a tip." There was a long pause, during which I suppressed a sigh of frustration.

"I think you should talk to Ariella Cantor, the art dealer, you know who she is anyway."

I took a moment to digest what Ian had said – what was he trying to tell me. Was I being dense here? I knew there was a link between Julia and Ariella, the earlier drama had proved that, but it was interesting that Ian – unprompted – had brought Ariella into the equation.

"Ian, listen, I'm not expecting you to breach a bond of trust, or break your word here, but what do you know about what's going on? I'm being blackmailed by one gangster, hunted by another set of gangsters, and on top of all that the police are looking for me, and it's all due to something I'm not even involved in." I stopped short of pleading, I couldn't allow myself to sink that low.

"Uh, not good, is it? I'm very sorry, Hugo, but I really don't know anything either – what a mess."

Ian stopped abruptly, and I could see that there was something he was wrangling with: to tell or not to tell. He looked away for a moment, and when he focused back, I could see he'd made up his mind. A thought hit me; did he know her real financial situation?

"Okay, Hugo. I'll tell you this: I was in line to put up the money for Julia on this game when she suddenly cut me off. It was Ariella Cantor, not Julia, who told me I was out." Ian slightly shook his head, displaying his misgivings about this way of conducting business. "I was disappointed, but I'm a big boy. It's more of a hobby for me anyway, I suppose. I always liked Julia. In my opinion she was always decent and conducted herself with integrity. I decided not to take offence, in business only the bottom-line counts. Even with friends. So, there you go, Hugo."

I was genuinely surprised. The fact that Ariella Cantor had been directly involved made this case even more complex. And I couldn't fail to notice that Ian had used the past tense when describing how he felt about Julia. Tapping my fingers on my leg, my mind was racing to compute this new information.

"Have you dealt with Ariella Cantor before?" I asked.

"Yes, but not in this sort of capacity. The walls of my office are adorned with art provided by her ...," Ian gestured towards a couple of big canvas oils in the room.

"Did she tell you who fronted the money?" I asked as I continued to take in the art works around me. The paintings themselves didn't interest me, but the link between Ariella and Julia did – more and more so.

"No, she didn't, and I didn't ask, nor did I dig to find out," Ian replied, and I knew he was talking about putting one of his guys onto that task. Ian had a small, but trustworthy in-house security team, who also investigated and did sensitive research at times. Ian invested in a lot of high-risk, high-tech start-ups, and liked to know the reality behind their sales patter and the truth about whom he was dealing with. I had also done jobs like that for him in the past. I made a mental note to see if I could have a quiet word with Bruno Holland, Ian's security chief. Bruno was a decent investigator in his own right and a guy I got on well with. He was the guy who had outsourced jobs to me in the past.

"Right, thanks, Ian. I really appreciate what you've told me. I think I'll go looking for Ariella. Do you mind if I come back to you if necessary?" I waited for Ian to walk around his desk.

"No problem, Hugo. And give Bruno a call any time. He's away on business just now, back tomorrow, but you can reach him on his mobile. Look after yourself. As I said, I've got another job for you, but it can wait." He extended his hand. I shook it and smiled. Sir Ian Keller was a good man.

"Bye for now, Ian. I'll get back to you," I said as I left his office.

Hitting the street, I pulled out one of my unregistered mobile phones and made a call.

"Good afternoon, this is the office of Ariella Cantor, Art Dealer. How may I help you?"

I didn't recognise the pleasant, French-accented voice.

"Good afternoon, this is Hugo Storm. Is Ariella Cantor available, please?" I felt sure I'd said this with just about the right amount of intensity to produce a positive result.

"Please hold."

The voice was replaced by classical music, which I guessed would be the music of choice for most of Ariella's clients. I waited anxiously and felt my stomach rumble.

"Ariella Cantor is busy just now, Mr Storm, but she can return your call in an hour."

"I see. Could I come to see her in an hour, in that case?" I wanted to look her in the eyes when broaching this subject.

"A moment please." There was another brief musical interlude before the pleasant voice returned. "Ariella Cantor can see you at 14.15, at the gallery."

"Thank you," I said, ending the call.

I glanced at my watch and saw that I had just over an hour to kill. My stomach rumbled again, reminding me that I was hungry; I couldn't recall when I had last eaten anything. My blood sugar was getting low and I needed to refuel, so I decided to grab something while I waited to see Ariella. I walked up the Royal Mile – it was busy with tourists and locals alike, meandering along this old street between Edinburgh Castle and Holyrood Palace. I decided on the Miles Pub, a big, old pub with a decent menu. A large portion of wholesome food was just what was required – though not so large that I would become sleepy. It was a place I visited now and again. Its heavy, dark interior was much like the city itself. Edinburgh: 'full of mystery and heavy on history, yet a city alive with a pulse and a vibe'. I liked that description of my favourite city. It was an atmosphere the Miles Pub had too.

I got myself a soft drink and another coffee as I ordered a steak pie with chunky chips. A portion of green peas covered the greens requirement. I chose a table for one next to a group of four slick-looking guys, all wearing dark suits. They looked like a bunch of lawyers having lunch together. I know a lot of lawyers – comes with the trade – but didn't recognise any of that group. Their conversation soon got my attention though: they were talking about the murder of the Norwegian poker player, and they were excited about it too. In front of me I had the day's edition of The Times. A couple of times one of the guys looked over at me, but I appeared to be immersed in the paper. I wasn't – I was all ears.

One of the younger guys seemed to have an inside track on the investigation, picked up from a family member of the hastily-gathered police task force. The family member had obviously been talking way too much, probably to impress. In turn, the lawyer guy was using the information to impress his colleagues at the table, particularly the oldest guy, the senior partner of the bunch, who I could tell was enjoying the tale spun by the hot young gun.

People talk, professionals talk. People gossip, and likewise professionals gossip. It's human nature, and no protocols, procedures, or professional standards will ever stop of band of colleagues, professional or otherwise, sharing 'war' stories or juicy gossip.

"Hugo, here's your lunch."

Heidi, the waitress, placed a large plate of steaming hot food in front of me. I looked up at the lanky brunette with a lovely smile and thanked her. I was aware that the mentioning of my name had abruptly halted the telling of the tale on the next table. They were all staring at me, which made sense since the hot young gun had just been saying that the police were looking for an infamous Edinburgh-based PI called Hugo Storm. Heidi quickly realised that she'd landed me in an awkward spot, but I smiled and reassured her.

"It's okay, Heidi – no worries."

She was about to reply but decided against it. With a flushed face she spun around and walked away. I waited until she disappeared through a staff-only door, then I looked over at the inquisitive faces at the next table.

"You guys got a problem?" I asked calmly, taking my time to eyeball each one of them. As I did, they all looked down, though the young chatterer held my stare for quite some time. I settled on the oldest guy, the senior one, and waited. He drew his head back in a gesture of embarrassment before meeting my eyes again. I saw a look of fear in his expression, as he searched for a suitable comeback. I waited, just holding his gaze while the others shifted uncomfortably in their chairs.

"No, Mr Storm, we don't have a problem here. I apologise for this. Please enjoy your meal." The man tried to smile but failed. I continued to glare at him for another moment, sending him a strong message before returning to my newspaper and meal. The guys held out for another four minutes, trying to overcome the awkwardness before draining off their drinks and making a hasty exit. I ignored them and focused on my lunch. I didn't have much time. I presumed the young guy with the look of defiance in his eyes would be on the phone to the police within seconds of leaving the pub. I wolfed down the meal, while looking out the windows fronting the Royal Mile. As expected, within five minutes a couple of uniforms appeared. I got up and quickly walked to the back of the big pub as if I was heading for the toilets, but then diverted through the staff-only door instead. Heidi looked up as I closed the door behind me. Another guy, a chef type, looked at me with surprise and was about to speak when Heidi raised her hand to silence him.

"I'm sorry Hugo, I didn't realise ..."

"Forget about it, Heidi. I just need to leave – pronto."

I gestured towards the front of the pub. Heidi looked at the door I'd just come through and understood immediately.

"Not a problem, Hugo. Through the door to the back, down the stairs and first right. Go through another door, then left and out through the back door into a close. Then you hit the back street. Okay?"

"Perfect. See you later."

I walked past the chef guy who wasn't too happy, but had wisely kept silent. These old buildings on the Mile were like a maze, with corridors, stairs and doors all at different levels. But Heidi had given me a path, and I quickly negotiated the maze and found my way out.

Back on the streets, I headed towards Princes Street. I needed a taxi. The police were obviously actively looking for me, so walking the streets was now too risky. Fortunately, there are plenty of taxis in Edinburgh, so I soon managed to flag one down and give the driver the address of my next port of call. Since it was only about a five-minute drive, the taxi driver gave me a funny look. I didn't explain, but just told him to drive.

FOURTEEN

The doorman was the type who could handle himself in brawl, but at this particular location he was required to be well-dressed and have excellent manners. He quickly blocked the door as I approached.

"Hi Gary, I'm looking for Ariella Cantor," I said calmly.

I knew the doorman well. He smiled but continued to block my entry.

"Mrs Cantor is unavailable." he said, a little too smugly.

Suppressing a flash of anger and the temptation to floor him, I said, "Listen pal, I need to see her now. I'm a bit early, but I'm sure she'll understand." I paused, met his eyes, and added, "Don't be an idiot now, Gary. I don't have time for games."

Gary lost the smug smile, took a moment to assess my intent, and smartly came to the logical conclusion: I was allowed to enter Ariella Cantor's art gallery, a very posh establishment in a posh building in a suitably posh part of Edinburgh. It was empty, no customers or staff, just Ariella Cantor herself waiting for me. She was standing by the counter, dressed in a tight-fitting, black outfit. She was slim, but still curvy, with shiny black hair framing her lush, tanned face. Simply gorgeous. Her slightly large nose and long, elegant neck gave her a majestic air. However, her large green eyes gave evidence of the turmoil she'd experienced over the past year and a half. Chloe Cantor, her little girl, was dead, but had never been found. Her little body, or what was left of it, was out there somewhere, and it was slowly tearing Ariella apart, piece by piece.

"Hugo, how nice to see you again," she said with a fragile voice, as she tried to smile. The effects of this effort at friendliness were clearly visible.

"Ariella, nice to see you again too," I said, and meant it. I couldn't help but feel an overwhelming sense of protectiveness towards her. The strength of this feeling, which I had felt before, nevertheless took me by surprise. Her proud, but so very fragile stance made me want to grab her and hold her tightly. I felt a strong urge to protect her, forever, from the big, bad world out there. Those feelings mixed uncomfortably with a sexual attraction towards her that I simply couldn't shift.

"Please, have a seat," she said as she gestured towards a smart bistro set.

"Thank you." I replied, sitting down on a metal-framed chair.

Ariella also sat down and pointed to a crystal decanter on the small table between us, saying, "Help yourself Hugo."

I looked at her as she glanced over at the front door. Was she expecting somebody? I decided not to let my conflicting feelings for her cloud my judgment. I had to assume she would play me, and I'd be a fool if I allowed that to happen. There was a link between her and Julia, but what it was still remained hidden.

"Well then, Hugo, tell me, how are you?" Ariella tried out her smile again – it worked better that time.

"Could be worse. How about you?"

A look of panic rolled over her eyes before she controlled herself and glanced away again. I realised that she must do that a lot – steady herself before feeling able to continue. Everything must be a battle, everything must just be draining.

"Oh, what can I say: I wake up, work, go home to a ghost house, then I wait for the phone call that will never come ..."

She looked at me and blinked, her lips tightly fused together. The obvious hurt in her words stung me right to the core. The bitterness took me by surprise, but then again it shouldn't have. How could anyone with a heart and soul not be in continuous pain if their child had been killed and their body never found. I didn't reply; there was nothing I could say.

Composing herself, she continued, "Sorry about that, Hugo. I just ..." Her emotions got the better of her; she stopped and shook her head, attempting to clear her thoughts yet again.

"Don't be sorry, it's okay," I said quietly as I reached out and touched her shoulder.

Her body jolted in response to my touch, as if struck by electricity, and her eyes revealed the hurt she felt as she tried again, "What can I help you with, Hugo?"

"I need to find Julia Felt – and urgently," I said.

Ariella didn't answer right away, but from the look in her big, fragile eyes, I saw that she knew where Julia was. "You're assuming I can help you with that?"

"Well, I hope you can," I pressed on, encouraged that she hadn't denied knowing Julia.

"It isn't that simple, Hugo, you know that."

She folded her arms across her chest in a defiant, defensive stand. Nonetheless, this was something I could work with.

"Yes, I can appreciate that, Ariella, but you know things are spiralling out of control fast. You heard what happened to Jens Brekken?" I paused and saw she had, then I continued, "I'm the least of her worries. There are others looking, and their agendas are not in Julia's interests."

"So, you're telling me your agenda is in her interest?"

There was a slight mocking tone to her voice. I didn't take offence; she probably didn't trust a living soul, and hadn't for quite some time. If I could convince her my intent was honourable then I believed she would talk.

"My agenda is in both Julia's and my interests, Ariella. I've been landed in a sticky situation here and I'm scrambling to get out of this in one piece. I'm not looking to cause Julia harm, I hope you can believe that. Whatever intention Julia had when getting involved in this, it's backfired – and badly."

I hoped the gravity of what I was saying would help Ariella to understand where I was coming from. I couldn't be sure of this, but I could at least hope.

"Who else is looking for her?" asked Ariella, tentatively, after having considered my words.

"Kenny Bullard, for one."

Ariella's large eyes were now pulsing with fear. Her non-verbal reaction told me she knew Kenny and that the prospect of his looking for Julia filled her with terror. She took a moment to recover before she was able to speak.

"Kenny Bullard is back?" Her voice was hushed, as she carefully put her glass down.

"Yes, he is, and it's not good. Not good for me obviously, but equally – I honestly believe this – not good for Julia either ..."

I was about to include Ariella herself in that statement but decided not to; the focus was on Julia. Judging by Ariella's reaction, she hadn't bargained for Kenny Bullard being part of the equation. It seemed that my bet had paid off. I didn't expect her to tell me where Julia was, or make a phone call whilst I was still sitting there, but I was sure she would make that call within a minute of my leaving. I decided to give her the opportunity, so I got up as if to go.

"You're leaving, Hugo?" Ariella jumped to her feet in surprise, wringing her hands in obvious anxiety.

I fished out a small notebook from my leather jacket, wrote down my number, tore off the page, and handed it to her. "Listen, I can be contacted on this number anytime – anytime, just call me."

Ariella searched my eyes for a long moment before looking down at the piece of paper. There seemed to be a sense of relief on her face as she looked at the number. It meant, I hoped, that she recognised me as a friend and not an enemy.

"Call me, Ariella – the quicker the better. For Julia's sake." I said as I turned to leave.

"Hugo!" Ariella's fragile voice stopped me in my tracks. She was holding onto the back of the chair, as though she needed to support herself.

"Yes?"

"Well ...," she paused, searching for her words. "Just wanted to say thank you, I guess. You take care, Hugo."

Ariella fell silent, maybe from the fear of saying too much, or maybe due to embarrassment? I wasn't sure what she was thanking me for, and I guessed she wasn't either. Perhaps it was part of her play, but it sure appeared genuine. I lifted a hand in a gesture of acknowledgement.

"Nothing to thank me for, Ariella. Just make the call." I left it at that and let myself out without looking back.

Gary was standing beside the door, but ignored me as I walked past him. I looked out at the street and saw a car, a grey Ford Focus, parked at the kerb. A tall, fit-looking woman dressed in a dark blue trouser suit and brown leather jacket was leaning against the front passenger door. As I stepped out onto the pavement, she pushed herself off the car and walked straight towards me, and a heavy-set guy in a suit stepped out of the Ford and walked around the vehicle.

"Hugo Storm?" she asked in a northern-England accent, as she reached for something inside her jacket.

"Yes, that's me," I said as I looked back at the woman. She was obviously the one in charge.

"Finally! You're a hard man to get hold of, Mr Storm. I'm Detective Sergeant Muller."

Her smile and her manner were somewhat aggressive as she presented me with her cop I.D. I inspected it and let out a sigh. If Ariella thought that having me off the street, would help Julia and her, she was dead wrong. But that didn't matter, now I had a problem and I needed to solve it as fast as possible.

"What can I do for you, Detective Sergeant?"

I studied her appearance. Combining what I saw with what I'd read about her gave me hope. Petite had fired over an email with information about this police officer before she'd shut up shop for the day. D.S. Muller glanced at her partner and flashed a predatory grin before focusing back on me.

"Mr Storm, you need to accompany us to the station. We have some questions for you."

"Do you have a warrant?" I asked, keeping my voice calm and my posture composed. I wasn't a lawyer, but I was very familiar with the law's tenets – essential knowledge in my line of work. Unless they had a warrant, I didn't have to go with them.

The female detective glanced again at her partner; her grin widened. I recognised the excited look of a predator in her expression. Without doubt she would relish a fight.

"Yes, in fact we do, and it would be in your own interests to come with us without any trouble. But it's up to you how we do this."

D.S. Muller's tone was aggressive as she stepped closer towards me. From her pocket she produced a document. I grabbed it and quickly scanned it: it was a warrant indeed, and genuine. I handed it back and looked her in the eyes. I was surprised to detect a hint of madness, and wondered what kind of copper she really was? I'd seen that look before, in soldiers during combat, stoked high on the premise of 'kill or be killed'. In the past, I'd also had that same look during my own combat experience. But with D.S. Muller it lay deeper; I could tell, it had seriously taken hold. This was a very dangerous individual.

"Calm down, no need for drama." I gestured towards the back door of the Ford, adding, "I'll come along, no worries."

Her partner, the big guy, moved up to my right side, and seemed equally stoked to get physical. His damaged eyes told me that he too was looking forward to some action. Who were this pair – the 'Lunatic Flying Squad'? The two coppers exchanged glances, both looked somewhat disappointed by my seemingly cooperative attitude. But, unbeknown to them, I was actually preparing myself to fight, loosening my shoulders and adjusting my balance. I was getting ready for the big guy – I could take him, I knew that, but that wasn't the point. I sensed he would come at me full throttle, with little control and even less skill. Then she would go nuts, and maybe she was armed. Fighting with cops is bad for business, and not something I would normally do, but the norm didn't apply here.

"All right, get in the back," D.S. Muller said flatly, gesturing towards the car.

"After you, Princess," the big fella said, with a hoarse laugh.

D. S. Muller laughed too. I walked to the car, with a red face, fighting the urge to turn and unleash my anger on them both. It felt like they were goading me to do just that, but I didn't take the bait. But boy did I want to! I opened the back door of the car and slotted myself in on the back seat. A smell of bleach and strong cleaning products hung heavily in the cab. The two coppers got into the car in quick succession, the big guy behind the wheel and D. S. Muller in the front passenger seat. She turned and looked at me as her partner pulled away from the kerb, not even bothering to put on her seatbelt.

"I've heard a lot about you, Hugo Storm. Not to mention your brother, Douglas. What a bad boy he is. You guys are legends." She laughed, her eyes exuding mayhem, still juiced. "Shame we have to meet under these circumstances."

A thought hit me – mention of my brother had made me think. These two were not protocol riders, not by a long shot!

"You want the killer of the Norwegian guy?" I stared intently at D. S. Muller.

"You gonna tell me you know who it is?" Her tone revealed her curiosity.

I shook my head, "No, not yet, but I know who I suspect." I studied her reaction. My apparent confidence made her pause, so I grasped my opportunity; there was no time to waste. I continued, "D. S. Muller, could you instruct your partner to pull in around the next corner."

She laughed, "Why, what a strange request. You think you can negotiate here?"

"Just indulge me. I can help you find the killer. And you and your colleague would get all the credit."

I stopped, allowing just enough time for this to sink in, but no more. I needed to keep the momentum going. D. S. Muller glanced at her partner whose blank expression I couldn't read. Scrambling now, feeling this was slipping away, I continued as the traffic in front of us ground to a halt, providing me with a little more time.

"I'm not involved in the murder of the Norwegian. You can waste time on me if you like, or you can keep looking. You know as well as me, the window for wrapping this up early is shutting fast. You used to serve in the Met, didn't you?"

D. S. Muller looked at me sharply and pointed a finger. "You're stepping way out of line here."

Her voice was laced with hostility, but I also detected a hint of fear; she knew that I knew about her past. My gut instinct told me she'd had to jump ship due to something bad. I didn't know the details, but just enough to convince her that I did. It was time to tighten the screws.

"Listen, D. S. Muller, I have no desire to use your secrets against you, but I will if I have to – and that includes disclosing your habit!"

I paused, steeling myself for an explosive reaction. The threat about disclosing her habit had been a gamble, but her reaction told me I'd hit the ball into the net. The world around us froze, and for a moment none of us seemed to breath. We just looked at each other. I read her eyes and knew my observations had been right: her dilated pupils, charged restless energy and the microscopic white flake I thought I could see beneath her right nostril confirmed my suspicion that she snorted cocaine. How often, and how much, I didn't know, but that was irrelevant. Some coppers use drugs, some drink, some gamble, some beat their partners, and a few, a very few, kill. They're human like the rest of us are, flawed, prone to making mistakes, and a few commit crimes due to temptation and lack of character. That's all information that somebody like me could use to get the upper hand. The bad ones I would shop right away, but somebody with a drug, alcohol, or gambling habit, or who was in the pocket of a gangster, I would keep to use as I saw fit.

"You scum ..." the voice of the big fella boomed.

D. S. Muller silenced him by raising her hand, and I ignored him as I continued to focus on D. S. Muller's eyes: rage, mixed with madness, danced wildly within.

"Clever. I'm impressed – guess what I've heard about you is right...," she paused and then without taking her eyes off me, said, "Pull over, Brian."

Her partner seemed about to protest but decided against it after she'd flashed him an authoritative look. With that sorted, she focused back on me.

"What do you want?" she asked in a voice like a compressed snarl.

"Give me forty-eight hours, just forty-eight hours, just back off from me and my assistant. That's all."

D. S. Muller screwed up her eyes in a concentrated squint as she considered my offer. I waited and waited, and the longer I waited, the more I became convinced that she'd go for it. It was noticeable that she didn't refer to her colleague: she was in charge here and would make this decision alone. Her partner would follow her lead, no questions asked, at least not in front of me. It didn't come easy, but I knew she'd give me what I wanted when I saw a film of resignation roll over her eyes.

Leaning in towards me in a conspiratorial manner she whispered in a low, hoarse voice, "Forty-eight hours, Hugo Storm. Not a minute longer, and then you contact me direct, understood? A warning: you'd better deliver!" She handed me her business card. I took it and saw that it was a simple Police Scotland card with her name, rank and mobile number only.

"I will, and thank you." I said, slipping the card into the inside pocket of my leather jacket as I quickly got out of the parked car.

Giving me a final, scrutinising look, she rolled down her window and said, "I can't stop my colleagues looking for you, and if you get caught you'd better not spin any fiction about me, or that would be outright suicidal for you ..." She paused, allowing her warning to sink in before continuing, "I'm doing you a huge favour here. Give me what I need, and you might be okay."

I didn't reply, just gave her a nod. She rolled up the window, and her partner drove off without any drama. I stood back on the pavement and watched as the car turned a corner. I couldn't quite believe it – that had been way too easy! I knew those two weren't riding the official train here, they had their own agenda.

"Join the ranks," I mumbled to myself.

Taking a breath, I looked around: the city of Edinburgh was going about its business as normal, on the surface at least. But as I knew, in the many dark, narrow alleys of this mysterious city, shadows were fending off other shadows in order to score. And this week more than usual. The big pot of money was out there, and every crook, with or without a badge, was scrambling to claim it. I broke into a grin, just another working week for me.

FIFTEEN

I secured a window seat in a 'trying-too-hard-to-be-hip' café on the other side of the street from Ariella Cantor's art dealership. From there I could keep an eye on the place as I nursed a glass of iced water. The café's corner location had enabled me to enter without being seen from the gallery. Gary had witnessed the incident with the coppers and had seen me driving away with them. He was no longer outside the gallery door; I guessed he'd be inside reporting this to Ariella. So, she would be thinking I'd driven away with the detectives. What would her next move be, I wondered? I believed she would contact Julia, and I hoped she'd go to wherever Julia was, thus leading me to her. That would be perfect. But I needed transport – and quick. I decided against using Harry, and called The Tap instead. The distinguished voice of Charlie Thomson greeted me.

"Charlie, I need a huge favour." I didn't have time to explain.

"Right, son - name it," Charlie replied without hesitation.

"You got your car outside?" I asked, anxiously tapping the table in front of me. I could try to hail a taxi if Ariella left right away, but that wouldn't be ideal. Edinburgh taxi drivers are used to strange instructions, but some might object to being asked to tail another car.

"Yes, do you need it, Hugo?"

"Yes, but I also need a driver, and I need both right away."

"Where are you?" Charlie asked.

"In a café, Art House Café, opposite Ariella Cantor's art gallery." I quickly calculated the time it would take Charlie to get here if he agreed.

There was a brief silence on his side, then, "Yes, I know it. Where do you want me?"

I smiled, he was a true friend – didn't need an explanation – just a call for help.

"Thank you, Charlie, can you come up Stoke Avenue? Park at the kerb as close to the entrance as you can. I'm watching Ariella's place from the café, I need to tail her if she moves."

"Give me five, Hugo."

I put the phone down on the table and felt excitement coursing through my veins. Damn. I couldn't help but love this, mess though it was, it was what I did. The minutes dragged on and I was getting restless. Three minutes had passed, though it felt like a lot longer. Gary came out of the front entrance in a hurry. He looked around before rushing down the street – I felt sure he was going to get Ariella's car. It would be parked in a side alley, two blocks away, where she had a designated parking space – at a premium in this part of Edinburgh. I glanced at my wristwatch, Charlie should be outside any minute now. This would be tight, but doable, and doable was as good as it got. Three minutes afterwards, a black Mercedes S-Class came to a sharp halt outside the gallery. I stood up, ignoring the looks of the people in the café. A waitress came up to me, I gave her a tenner.

"I gotta go – here, keep the change," I said without looking at her.

Across the street Ariella was leaving. She closed the door and strode across to the waiting Mercedes. It was time to move.

Charlie was indeed outside, engine running, parked neatly just outside the front door. At least something was working out for me. I ran around the back of Charlie's Jaguar and got into the front passenger seat.

"She's on the move in a black Mercedes S-Class. I don't know where she's headed, but the car's pointing in our direction." I'd calculated that there were three possible ways the Mercedes could go: first, an illegal U-turn; second, across from us towards the city centre; or third, straight down past us.

"Right, Hugo, I'll pull out, if she's coming our way then we should see the car in just a few seconds," Charlie said as he quickly drove forward to the intersection.

"Thanks Charlie," I said as I glanced over and saw the sparkle in his eyes. It wasn't just me getting excited here. Charlie with his brown leather driving gloves, of course, simply liked a good thrill like the rest of us.

Coming up to the intersection, we saw the Mercedes indeed doing a U-turn. Charlie didn't hesitate, he pulled out and turned to follow it keeping a cautious distance. Tailing a vehicle in a city is a complicated matter. In a perfect tail a driver would manage to keep other vehicles between the target and himself, but in city traffic that would almost guarantee losing the tail. Almost was the operative word here. Follow immediately behind the target, and one would be noticed. It was a trade-off. Charlie let another car come in between us as we followed the Mercedes through another intersection.

"How complicated is your situation?" Charlie asked with his eyes focused ahead.

"Very. Yesterday I was blackmailed to find Julia Felt – she's in hiding. That was before I found out that Jens Brekken had been killed, and I assume his prize money is missing as well. Then I found out Kenny Bullard is back and looking for me. And not long ago, I had an encounter with what can only be described as two dirty detectives – what their agenda is, I'm not sure ..." I paused and took a breath. It didn't sound good.

"All right, a complicated situation indeed," Charlie said, navigating the Jaguar through another intersection as he focused on tailing the car in front.

We'd been lucky with traffic so far and although Gary was driving aggressively, Charlie was managing to keep up. And by the looks of it, no-one in the Mercedes was aware of us.

I laughed at his deadpan reply, "Indeed."

"Well, I was wanting to talk to you, Hugo – the buzz in the shadows is at an all-time high."

"Yes, I'm all ears, Charlie." I knew Charlie was well connected.

"Right, as far as I can tell by what I've heard, the money's missing. The speculation is that Julia's got it. That's the number one theory," he paused, giving me time to digest what he'd said.

"That's what I've been thinking too, but would Julia be involved in a murder robbery?"

I was asking myself more than Charlie. I was having a hard time believing it, but I didn't know the circumstances, maybe she hadn't signed up to the murder. I reminded myself of my core rule: never rule anything out when it comes to people – even those considered to be friends – one never really knows anyone. Charlie didn't say anything, letting me mull over my thoughts. I was grateful for that, so much had happened in so little time, I needed time to process it all.

Road works up ahead brought the Mercedes to a standstill. Luckily a big SUV had slotted itself between us, so we weren't worried about being spotted.

"You know as well as me that you never know, Hugo. But I heard an interesting piece of information that turns this around: one theory goes that Kenny Bullard is involved in the murder, as in that he ordered the murder." Charlie's face was serious and focused as he spoke.

I shot a glance back at him. That made sense, a lot of sense. And it possibly changed the game for me too; now my question was whether I was a piece in Kenny's game?

"Interesting piece of information, Charlie. May I ask from whom you got that?"

Charlie looked at me – he wasn't the type to name his sources, that was his code. Thus, people trusted him. Whatever it was, it stayed with Charlie. I'd challenged him here, maybe even crossed the line.

"You shouldn't ask me that, Hugo, but yes you're entitled to know," Charlie paused, "I was told this yesterday evening by Ricky Slapper."

Charlie focused back on the road as we got a green light. I knew of Ricky Slapper, a former building contractor of dubious quality who was now heavily involved in equally dubious payday-loan finance. He was a loan shark who lent small amounts of money to desperate people, at steep weekly interest rates. I didn't like him, he was a bragging sleazebag with no moral compass.

"Why did Ricky tell you this?" I asked.

Charlie gave me a knowing look and answered, "Because he likes to be considered important. He was having a drink with Jake Munro at the bar. They were talking about the murdered Norwegian. Ricky couldn't help himself."

Jake Munro was another white-collar crook on the shady side of the Edinburgh business community, but he was smarter than Ricky, and generally pleasanter too. As far as I knew, Jake didn't rip off desperate single mothers or vulnerable old age pensioners. His speciality was online fraud, perpetrated against stupid, wealthy clients, mostly inheritance types with money to burn on 'get-even-richer-quicker' pyramid schemes. Jake had managed to avoid jail, every case so far had been easy for Jimmy Johnson to shred to pieces. Thinking of Jimmy, maybe Charlie had some intel on him too. But I needed to explore Ricky more; had he just been spinning a tale or was there substance to what he claimed?

"Yeah, I totally get that he did that to look important to Jake, but do you think there's anything to what he said? Is he in business with Kenny?" I said.

Charlie nodded in agreement.

"Yes, I know Ricky is flipping payday loans with Kenny's backing. They're a good match, they'd rip off their own mothers if money could be made. And Ricky said Kenny's back." Charlie focused on the traffic ahead before continuing, "And I don't know if you know this, but he partially blames you for that forced exile to Spain."

I looked ahead, this was making sense, a lot of sense. Kenny neither understood nor accepted the affinity his father had for me. Kenny had been 'exiled' to Spain due to an event that I'd only had a very minor part in.

"I wasn't the reason Cameron had forced Kenny to relocate to Spain; Kenny himself was the reason for that."

"Yes, but I don't think Kenny sees it that way... or put it this way, he doesn't want to see it that way. The man needs somebody to blame, most people do," Charlie said in a matter-of-fact way as he glanced over at me.

I shrugged, I knew Charlie was right – it didn't matter what I thought, Kenny considered me an enemy, end of. I looked in the wing mirror and noticed a car I'd seen earlier: a grey BMW, an older model-3 series. It was hanging back, keeping its distance – I'd seen it before, twice.

"Charlie, I think we have a tail."

"Roger that. We're tailing Ariella and somebody's tailing us. Do you want to lead whoever's behind us to Ariella's destination?" Charlie checked his mirror. "The grey BMW, you think?"

"Yes, I've seen it twice," I replied, as I considered Charlie's question. It was a good question. I was thinking Julia Felt was in on this, on Kenny's team, but now I was developing doubt. Maybe she'd been initially involved, but had then bailed out, for whatever reason. Kenny wasn't the type to say, 'you had a change of mind, never mind.'

"And in reply to your previous question: no, not until I can figure out who's who in this game. I don't want Ariella hurt," I said whilst keeping an eye on the car behind.

"All right," Charlie said.

Easing off the speed, we let another car pull in front of us and drove through the next junction. Looking back, I saw the BMW take a right-hand turn and disappear, then another car took its place: a dark blue Ford Mondeo. I was certain I'd seen it too a couple of times earlier.

"They're doing parallels: two cars working together, at first a grey BMW 3-series and now a dark blue Ford Mondeo," I said, unable to conceal my admiration of their trade craft. If it was Kenny's crew, then they had certainly honed their professionalism. That didn't bode well for me in this game.

"Well, it might not matter – something's spooked Ariella, or her driver at any rate," Charlie shook his head as he spoke.

Staring ahead, I saw the Mercedes blow right through a red light in front of us, causing a van to honk aggressively in protest at such a near miss. A thought hit me and I fished out my mobile.

"I am going to contact Petite, and see if she can hack the system and trace that Mercedes. If she can, we can lose this tail and then get to where we're going."

"Interesting. I'll find a place to park, an awkward place for our own tail – we'll see then what they do. You just call Petite," Charlie urged, and drove straight on as the light turned green.

Charlie was in his late fifties, but he wasn't a technophobe as so many of his generation were. In fact, I'd never heard him even once trot out the hackneyed cliché about things all being so much better 'back in the day'. He seemed to totally appreciate how useful modern technology could be, even though he didn't understand it himself.

"Just out of curiosity, how will she trace the Mercedes?" Charlie asked as he pulled into the centre of the road, slotted the gear in park and put the hazard-warning lights on. The road was wide at that section, so there was ample room for traffic to pass us in both directions.

"By hacking into its GPS tracker. That's how Kenny traced me, I believe."

I saw the Mondeo driving past us, with Mike Cunningham in the front passenger seat. He didn't look away, just gave us a mean stare.

"Clever – very twenty-first century ...," Charlie chuckled and said, "Mike doesn't look too happy, does he?"

"Twenty-first century – spot-on, Charlie! And Mike sure doesn't."

At that moment, I heard Petite's voice as she answered my call.

"Hugo, what's up?"

"Can you talk?" I asked as I leaned over, tapped Charlie on his shoulder and said, "Charlie, let's follow Mike and see what happens."

Charlie wasn't worried about Kenny by the looks of it. But then again, he was a well-established and respected figure in Edinburgh society, who even Kenny would hesitate to move against. Charlie found an opening in the traffic and shot the Jaguar into it. Up front the Mondeo was taking a left turn.

"Hugo, what's going on." Petite's voice brought my focus back to the phone in my hand.

"Sorry, I'm with Charlie, and we were tailing Ariella Cantor. She's involved all right ... anyway it's a long story. So, I gather you can talk?"

"Yes, I'm at home. Your office-combo flat has been sealed off by the police. Hugo, you haven't heard, have you?" Petite's voice was intense.

"No – heard what?" My heart was in my mouth – what was Petite about to tell me?

"Cameron Bullard has been murdered. His body was found somewhere down by the docks. Killed in very much the same way as Jens Brekken, my source-in-the-know tells me. It hasn't hit the news yet, the discovery and the location are not common knowledge, so the police don't need to worry about it becoming viral on the net or anything."

I didn't react, just stared incredulously at Charlie, who'd also heard Petite's words – we were both too stunned to speak.

SIXTEEN

When a bad plan unravels, it tends to unravel badly, and this was looking more and more like a bad plan. The problem, first and foremost on my mind, was that people were being killed here and I couldn't help but wonder if I'd be next. Somebody was killing in a professional manner, with a body count of two that I knew about so far. Professional killings in Scotland were almost unheard of. Gangster warfare did happen, but it was mostly amongst the lower ranks, amateur stuff, messy, and usually confined to street-level turf and deal disputes. A professional killer taking out senior-level people was something extraordinary.

I was about to voice my thoughts, when Charlie pulled aside and stopped tailing Mike. There was a very serious look on his face and I could see that for him the fun had stopped. He had just realised that if a boss like Cameron could be killed, then nobody was safe, neither him nor me.

"This changes things, Hugo," Charlie said as he tapped the wheel with a gloved hand and considered the magnitude of what we'd just heard.

I didn't reply at first, just looked out the front window whilst doing my own thinking. Cameron Bullard gone! It was such a momentous thought to deal with. He had dominated the criminal underworld in Scotland for decades. His reach had been far and wide, often surprising those who were arrogant enough to believe they could outplay him. I'd got to know him quite well and for the most part I'd managed to even like the guy. Obviously, there'd been times when I'd hated him, and even though we'd established a kind of rapport that his children didn't much approve of, fear was always present when in Cameron's company. A part of me was relieved he'd gone, because I knew that sooner or later, he would've come for me. I started thinking about who would've wanted him dead, when Charlie verbalised what I was thinking.

"If this was Kenny's work, then he's certainly gone mad. This kind of killing spree might work in a Godfather movie but not here in Scotland. The police will be throwing everything they've got at this, the Bullard organisation will be shredded, one way or another. Problem is, will anybody else die before this mess is stopped?"

"Agree, Petite told me Chris Lafferty's in charge of the task force and now he wants to talk to me. And, there was something else Petite told me ..."

"You want to share it, Hugo?"

"Detective Sergeant Rachel Muller, who waited for me outside Ariella Cantor's gallery earlier and then bizarrely let me go after I threatened to expose her secret, has a warrant out on Ariella."

Charlie whistled and said, "The plot thickens, Hugo. Who is this Detective Sergeant Muller, other than presumably a crooked copper?"

"A loose cannon who snorts cocaine and resigned from the London Met. last year due to some drama, but somehow managed to join Police Scotland." I gasped as I thought about Julia and Ariella: they were in deep trouble here, maybe deservingly so, but not enough to be killed. This was getting truly out of hand.

"Charlie, I understand if you want to walk away from this mess. This has got nothing to do with you – but I do need a car. I want to find Julia and find out what the blazes is going on. Not to mention why Kenny's coming after me."

"Hugo, my good friend, I'm now very much involved in this. We need this sorted, somehow, before I can go to sleep without worrying about Mike Cunningham or any of his associates coming for me in the middle of the night."

I assumed Mike knew that the Jaguar he was following belonged to Charlie Thomson. Anyway, when he passed us, he definitely clocked Charlie in the car with me.

"Right then, shall we drive to the address Petite traced the Mercedes to? It's currently at a standstill, but Petite will let me know if it moves." I said and looked at Charlie. Charlie took a moment, processing fast before nodding.

I felt relieved: just now it felt good to have a partner by my side. Charlie wasn't a young buck any more, but he was a smart fella who'd been around the block a few times. If it came to a fight, I could take care of that, but having a street-wise operator like Charlie Thomson at my side was nothing but an asset.

"Let's go. You guide me. Is it far?" Charlie asked and slotted the gear lever into drive.

"No, not far at all, ten minutes driving perhaps. Did you see the left turn Mike's Ford took?"

"Yes. So, you think they've done the same thing?"

"Well, they hacked my tracker or sat-nav. They could've hacked Ariella's car, or even placed a physical tracker on it."

"Okay, why were they tailing us and trying to stay hidden?" Charlie asked as he floored the accelerator of the big cat.

"I don't know." I replied.

"Many elements to this puzzle, Hugo," Charlie replied as he navigated the car efficiently through the traffic.

I just nodded, the man was right. I focused back on the map on my smart phone, as it guided us towards the destination. There was a sense of excitement in the air between us.

"Take a right at the next junction, Charlie, and then pull over. The destination is down this street on the right."

"Sure thing," Charlie replied in a low, intense voice.

Charlie turned at the next junction, found a spot on the right and neatly slotted the Jaguar next to the kerb of the quiet residential street.

Large detached homes lined the street on both sides; they were up-market new builds, a mix of similar designs, each with a driveway and neat, unfenced lawns to the front. In this part of Edinburgh suburbia they would each be worth a cool half million, give or take: the homes of well-paid professionals, with large mortgages, but little time.

"Listen, Charlie, I'll get out, but you stay put in the car ready to go. My phone's on silent, but call me if you see anything I need to know – vibrate is on. I'll come back, or call you when I know what's going on here."

Charlie hesitated for a moment before he asked, "You armed?"

"No, what about you – you got a piece in the car?"

I didn't carry, the police had refused to renew my gun licence five months ago. After a failed challenge, I'd duly handed in my registered 9mm Glock, but made sure my unregistered Beretta 9mm was hidden and secure. Using a gun in Scotland, or anywhere in the UK for that matter, was normally a complete no-no for anybody aiming for a sustained career in my field. But this was different. People were being killed here and I'd rather take a jail sentence than end up dead.

"Yes, in the boot, in a hidden compartment. A hunch told me it could come in handy. It's not registered, but it's clean. You want it?"

Charlie stared straight at me and I could see that he was deadly serious. The man had grown up in Kingstown, Jamaica, where teenagers haul assault rifles about. A hand gun was no big deal.

I only needed to think about for a few seconds, then said, "Yes, I'll take it – just in case."

"Okay, it's under the floor, here's the key."

Charlie knew there was no need for a lecture, I'd served in the British Army, and was proficient with firearms. I took the key and looked back at him; his eyes told me what I needed to know. Charlie was helping me here, but he was not going down as a co-conspirator on a murder charge. If it turned messy then I would be on my own. Fair enough.

"Thank you, Charlie."

I got out of the car, stood on the pavement and took a moment to scan the street. Up front there was a right-hand bend and my target was behind the curve, out of sight. It was just another Tuesday afternoon in just another working week; the schools were finished for the day, and suburbia was coming alive with kids and families. No way would I start blasting here, but I decided to take the gun anyway. I walked round to the boot, satisfied myself that nobody was watching, then quickly opened it. Using the boot as a shield, I unlocked the compartment, located and checked the weapon and dropped it in a sturdy, small, black, man-bag. I closed the boot and crossed the street behind the Jaguar, ignoring Charlie inside. I walked at a normal pace, carrying the bag at my side with the strap across my shoulder. I was exposed but that couldn't be helped. Sometimes one just had to make a move and throw the dice.

This wasn't where Ariella lived – unless she'd moved – and I couldn't remember reading anything about Julia's affairs that had included this location. But Julia had friends, people who would protect and help her. Sometimes the best way to hide was in plain sight. My phone started to buzz in my pocket and I cursed under my breath. Withheld number. "Damn!" I whispered. To answer or not to answer? That was the question in the twenty-first century. I decided I needed to answer, it could be something important.

"Hugo, you there?"

"Yes, what's up, Tam?" I asked, sensing a certain dread forming in my stomach.

"It's about Claire and Emily," Tam continued, his tone telling me something was amiss.

I steeled myself. My kids were my weak spot, the thought of harm coming their way freaked me out. I don't care how tough a person claimed to be, if he had a soul, even a fractured one, the thought of his children being harmed should affect him.

SEVENTEEN

"They're on the move. Claire's packed the car up for what looks like a long drive. What do you want us to do?" Tam's voice was urgent as he updated me on the latest situation.

I let out a sigh, relief washed over me like a wave. Claire was a capable woman, who was taking charge of what she could control. She and Emily were getting out of town. I didn't blame her.

"Don't interfere, Tam, but follow her. Make sure she and Emily get away safely. Let me know where they're going."

I noticed a car coming up behind me. A guy in a silver Audi A5, white shirt, groomed hair, home from the office. He glanced over at me as he rolled past, a brief and blank glance, didn't seem interested. Good, not somebody I needed to worry about.

"Sure thing, Hugo ...," Tam paused for a moment, then continued, "You okay, Hugo?"

"Yes, I'm getting this sorted," I said somewhat half-heartedly. But I told myself that I had to get this sorted, somehow!

"I'll get back to you, Hugo. Gotta run brother."

Tam had picked up the tone in my voice, but decided he didn't want to explore it further. I could appreciate that. I brought my focus back, launched Google maps on my phone and switched to street-view. Around the bend was where the Mercedes should still be parked. The location in question was a detached villa of standard design, the same as the others in the street, with a double drive on one side leading up to a detached double garage. A stone wall fronted the property towards the street. It would be difficult to approach the house without being in plain view. I could try to sneak in from behind, but there were houses there as well. It was afternoon, people were coming home from school and work, and being caught in somebody's back garden was not what I wanted, particularly as I was carrying a weapon. I took a breath and shifted my balance back and forth. I felt the restlessness in my neck taking hold. I was tired of being a pawn in someone else's game of chess. It was time to shake this up.

I put the phone away and began walking purposefully. I instantly started to feel better, being proactive instead of reactive was a mindset thing for me. Being in control, making the moves was the way I preferred to do business. Adrenaline was racing through my veins as I walked around the bend. I consciously loosened my shoulders and fingers, and continued to walk briskly towards the house in front of me. There were four cars outside the property, two of which were on the drive, including Ariella's Mercedes. The two cars that had tailed Charlie's Jaguar were parked at the kerb, with the Mondeo blocking the drive.

Gary was an amateur, he had no finesse; unless he rammed the cars on the kerb he was stuck. I shook my head in disbelief. With the money Ariella had, one would think she would employ better quality staff. I scanned the house as I crossed the street. A guy at the front door saw me, had a good look, then quickly disappeared inside. Well, this was it then: they would now know I was coming. Fine. I didn't care, I was doing this to shake things up, and shake things up I would.

"Get ready boys, here I come," I mumbled under my breath, as I rushed up the drive with a spring in my step. By now the energy was bouncing through my body. I felt strong and invincible, my senses were fine-tuned, my muscles straining to explode, my power ready to unleash. I was in fight mode.

The way one wins a fight is one half mindset, one quarter skill and one quarter strength. Even being outnumbered, I felt confident I could deliver enough hurt early on to gain the upper hand. And I was armed. Even most gangsters are smart enough not to argue with a gun. The bag was unzipped and the gun in my hand, as I took the four steps in two strides.

EIGHTEEN

They were waiting for me inside the hall: two guys, one of whom turned out to be Gary. I didn't hesitate as I kicked the door in and charged holding the gun in my right hand. In Scotland guns are rare, even amongst gangsters. Gary's eyes widened as he saw the weapon, and both guys lost their smug confidence. The hall was a confined space, which by its very nature would give an advantage to the man making the moves. Momentum ruled. I used my gun as a club and hit Gary hard to the head: he went down – lights well and truly out. The second guy shook off his initial paralysis and came for me, but he was too late. I rammed him hard into the wall, making the big mirror come crashing down, winding him. While he was incapacitated, I kneed him in the privates and then landed a blow to his jaw with the butt of my gun as he folded forward. He went down with a guttural grunt of pain. I stepped over the two of them and proceeded into the house.

"You want to put that gun down, Hugo."

Mike Cunningham spoke from behind my back, stopping me in my tracks. I looked over and straight into the barrel of Mike's pistol. He was about six feet away, too far for me to make a move without him having time to pull the trigger. And he wouldn't miss from there.

"Sure," I replied, putting the gun down at my feet.

Mike gestured with his gun, then said, "You just continue straight ahead to the living room, Hugo. Make sure you step over the gun now."

I did as he said. Storming in as I'd done wasn't perhaps the wisest move, but I didn't care. I was confident I could get out of this situation, that an opportunity would present itself. In the army, during my operational tours, I'd done similar 'stunts' as my superiors had labelled them

– one of the reasons they'd kicked me out. But I'd done so to shake things up, always having first considered the possible escape routes. There were risks attached to every situation.

"My man, Hugo, you sure know how to make an entrance!"

Kenny Bullard laughed as I walked into the dark living room. He was back. Kenny was square and fat, fatter than I remembered him being. Guess those cocktails in Spain had never stopped coming. Not a handsome guy, the gene mix between his mother and father had not been an aesthetic success. He looked scary, unhinged and angry, which in a strange way suited the man.

I didn't respond, but took a quick look around. The room was sombre, with heavy, dark leather and wood furniture. Some ventilation wouldn't have gone amiss; the air was more than a little stale, probably because the windows were all closed, as were the blinds. Further back Sheila Collins was standing, smoking in a stressed manner, she looked away as I shook my head in disgust.

I focused back on Kenny. He was sitting in an armchair, legs apart, with his big belly hanging heavily between. He appeared to be calm and relaxed, but his eyes were alight from the violence he'd heard in the hallway. That was Kenny all right, the man simply got off on violence, always had, always would. Sitting on the edge of a similar chair on the other side of a small, round coffee table was Ariella. Her big eyes, wider than I could remember ever having seen them, shifted about as she darted anxious looks at me. She was alarmed for sure, but as I read the scene I realised that the cause was not what I'd expected. She was alarmed by my arrival, not by having to keep company with Kenny. I would come back to her, but for now I returned my focus to Kenny. He was looking at Ariella, and a smug smile had started to spread across his face as he too read the alarm in her eyes. I modified my opinion. Ariella wasn't here because she wanted to be, she was here because she needed to be.

"Long time no see, Kenny. What are you playing at?"

I looked him right in the eyes and saw deeply ingrained evil in his squint expression. If there was ever need for evidence that some were indeed born evil, Kenny would be exhibit number one. The man had been outright evil even as a child, displaying the classic signs, such as torturing animals, which escalated through bullying and violence as he grew up. I'd heard that even his old man had balked at some of the things this son had done.

"Yeah, it's been a long time. And you don't know how much I've been looking forward to this moment. Your brother in the slammer, and you running around like a headless chicken. Your world just collapsing around you ..."

Kenny slapped his left thigh and started to laugh, a laugh that came from the deep, making his big belly pump up and down. No doubt the man was really enjoying himself. I felt my face going hot with anger, but I didn't respond. 'Let him indulge himself in his triumph,' I silently told myself. His arrogance and vanity would make him tell me what I needed to know. Kenny was the type who loved to brag, he'd always been like that. He was the big man who always won, was always the best, and never lost. However, nothing about that was true; I knew that and those around him knew it too. But he was Cameron Bullard's oldest and thus heir to a wealthy criminal empire, so those around him went along with the fantasy. His father not so much, but he was now dead.

"Why are you doing this?" I asked as I lowered my eyes.

It was time to play the slain opponent and enable Kenny to continue polishing his crown. His laughter stopped and I looked up. My eyes weak, my shoulders dropped, wringing my hands, looking suitably pathetic – I hoped. Kenny was grinning from ear to ear. Ariella appeared to be passively shrinking where she sat, as she continued to look down; seemingly resigned to her fate, whatever that might be.

"Why do you think, Hugo? Because of you I've been in flamin' exile for two years! Many people like Spain, but I don't. It's too hot for starters, and it isn't home," Kenny paused, losing the grin, his face shifting to pure fury, "My father took your side, against me and sent me away. Damn you, Hugo!"

Kenny stopped, and helped himself to the bottle of beer on the table. His anger was so strong it could almost be felt. I knew it wasn't my fault he'd been sent away, and his father certainly hadn't asked me what to do with him, but I also knew there was no point in arguing this. It would only stoke his anger further, and Kenny simply lacked brakes. I was walking a fine line here.

A man's delusional lie if fuelled by anger, hate or grievance will soon become a truth in his own mind. That's how populist politicians manipulate voters, and how individuals manipulate others, even themselves. Nothing is stronger than a belief based on grievance, be it real or not, and it's much easier to swallow than accepting difficult facts and taking responsibility. And Kenny never took responsibility.

I waited, letting him burn out the peak of his fury, hoping he would calm himself down and continue to talk. If he wasn't side-tracked or stoked, then I anticipated the odds were decent for that to happen. Luckily nobody said anything, not even Mike, who I could sense behind me. Kenny's fits of rage were legendary; blending into the background was considered the best option when they happened. But I knew now, this was personal with Kenny. I'd suspected it, but I hadn't realised how passionate he felt about it, until now. It was good to know. Now I just needed to survive this and get away. I was still working on that.

"You know my father is gone? Rest in Peace, old man. I'm now in charge and things are going to change around here, Hugo. Mark my words."

The fury had burnt itself out and the smirk was back. I made sure my inner happiness wasn't visible. Time to progress this.

"Who robbed and killed this Norwegian guy then, and why?" I asked

There was a pause as Kenny considered my question. It was a risky one, since I believed that it hadn't all gone according to plan. It could flare him up again. I looked up with what I considered to be a suitably wounded expression and saw that Kenny was scrutinising me.

Breaking into his smug signature grin, he said, "That would be you, Hugo. You did it for the money, or maybe revenge. Anyway, who cares?" Kenny looked over at Ariella, as if seeking her appreciation of his cleverness.

"You sure it'll stick, Kenny?" I was testing how well he'd worked this story out. The whole thing was a bit of a shambles – but that was Kenny. His plans in the past had often turned sour, leaving a total mess behind. No reason that should've changed. That was mainly why his father had dragged his heels on stepping aside and giving Kenny the top spot: the guy was simply a disaster jockey. However, it also meant it was unhealthy to get caught up in his ventures. One would get burned; it was just a matter of timing and severity.

Kenny didn't seem to appreciate my questioning his fantastic plan, and his face went red with anger. But then he surprised me: he didn't blow a fuse. Instead he said, "Listen, Hugo, I'm making this stuff up as I go along – it's a plan in development. Sure, this is a mess, but it could be worse. What I hadn't expected was another crew with their own plans ..."

He paused and glanced at Sheila before he looked over at Ariella. I followed his gaze. Ariella didn't react, just sat there, looking down. Now, there'd been two competing plays going on here. This Jens fella was victim number one. What about Julia? Julia, Jens, Sheila, Angus and Ariella had been working together, not realising, I guessed, Kenny was back with his own agenda.

Kenny cleared his throat, smiled, and continued, "You will be found with the murder weapon on you. Your prints will be on the weapon, and most importantly you will be incapable of professing your innocence as you will be dead."

It was quite a speech, especially for Kenny, and showed interesting insight, reflection and outright pragmatism. I was impressed. Kenny too was pleased with it; his mean grin positively oozed pride.

"Right, but who really did it? And why? Why not humour a doomed man?"

"Oh, we're just waiting for her, you arrived at the right time, really. She'll bring the murder weapon. It's all finally falling into place. Neat – I like neat! It was Mike's suggestion, you know – when things all started going south, he said, 'Let's stick it on Hugo! He can't help himself; he'll follow the scent like a dog tracking down a bitch on heat.' And you sure did! Of course, it helped that Angus gave you a push too. Proper team effort this."

Kenny pointed to my face, his hand shaped like a gun. A chuckle behind me told me that Mike was enjoying this too. I suppressed the urge to turn and wipe the smile off his face. Ariella, however, was not enjoying any of it; she, was utterly deflated. Kenny noticed my glance at her and was keen to prolong this moment of triumph.

"Ariella Cantor, our mutual friend – I did business with her brother-in-law, that is until you crashed that. You, Hugo, always you. Anyway, these fools thought they had the perfect plot. Score millions and head for the Caribbean or wherever; the game fixed, money guaranteed. But it just didn't quite work out that way. I understand the desire to scheme against my father, but it almost blew up what I had planned. But first Angus, then Sheila and finally Ariella, all scrambling. Ariella last, called me begging ... and brought you to me. All willing to trade ...The rats turning on each other, beautiful!"

Kenny leaned over and laid a hand on Ariella's shoulder; she noticeably winced at his touch. The evil in Kenny's eyes glowed brighter as he saw and felt her reaction. I could see fear in her eyes – fear in its truest form. I didn't speak, I was absorbing Kenny's every word. I couldn't help but be intrigued: two plays had clashed. The unfortunate thing was that Kenny's was the winner.

"Right then, Kenny – you seem to have this wrapped up. But you don't have Julia, and you don't have the money ...," I paused and smiled. Now I wanted to provoke him; angry people make mistakes. That was something I could testify to. I wanted him spitting anger. It worked. Kenny got up, the fury was venting from him as he stepped towards me. Bad move.

"Kenny...," Mike said from behind me, alarm in his voice.

Kenny looked over, and with that gave me the opening I'd been waiting for. I moved in, flung my right arm out and around his throat. As I swung him around, I reached for my blade with my left hand. Mike didn't shoot immediately – another mistake – and within a few seconds I had Kenny in front of me, as a human shield. I'd counted on Mike's having grown complacent, his hitman days for Cameron were long gone.

Although fat and heavy, Kenny was still strong – but not strong enough. I had him in a grip which gave me control. He should've dropped to the floor, which would've exposed me, but instead he followed his instinct and fought to remain on his feet. With him in front of me, and the other hesitating, I pushed Kenny hard, straight towards Mike. Neither had expected that and both were off balance. Kenny stumbled, instinctively reached out and grabbed Mike. I followed close behind, with the knife at the ready. Mike stepped backwards, attempting to avoid being caught by Kenny's considerable mass.

"Scumbag...," Mike shouted, and fired. The sound of the shot was overwhelming in the room, but Mike's aim was off, and the bullet removed a piece of Kenny's ear as it flew past me. Kenny finally lost his footing, and to further aid his fall I kicked him hard in his back. Kenny grabbed Mike as he stumbled forward. Mike dropped his gun and fell backwards with Kenny on top. Kenny holding onto him with a vice-like grip, screaming and bleeding. Mike fell hard, hitting the back of his head against the tiled floor with a sickening thud.

They thought they had it under control, but within a few seconds the tables had turned. That's how it goes. If one wants to control people, the number one rule is to stay out of their reach. Mike was a gangster, but he wasn't a professional gun slinger; I had counted on his hesitating to fire when the time came, and my gamble had paid off. I stepped over their vanquished bodies, dropped my knife into my leather jacket pocket and bent down to pick up both guns, Suddenly, Ariella jumped up from her chair and bolted past me.

NINETEEN

A scream, resonating desperation and fear, followed by a gunshot, rang out from the hall. With a weapon in each hand I moved rapidly over to the wall, aiming the gun in my right hand at the living room door. I waited. The scream had come from Ariella. I assumed she'd been shot. Somebody could've entered the room during those last chaotic moments, or perhaps the goons out front had become operational again? I waited, calming my pulse and breathing, and crouched down, making myself as small a target as I could be. I still had the gun aimed, and was in balance, ready to spring into action.

"Hugo, you ..." Kenny cursed me colourfully as he sat himself up. He'd rolled off Mike's lifeless body and was sitting staring at me with eyes full of hatred. His hair and clothing were badly dishevelled, and blood was running down his neck, soaking his clothes.

"What the hell's going on in there?"

I recognised the calm, controlled voice of Detective Sergeant Muller coming from the hall. So, she was the killer. She was the one Kenny had been waiting for. Now I understood why I'd been released: D. S. Muller was a killer cop with nothing left to lose, nothing more than that. How she'd got to that point I neither knew nor cared. They wanted me here to finish me off and arrange the end game. Well, I'd just changed their end game – but I wasn't home and dry just yet. In fact, the stakes had now been raised because this particular shooter would not hesitate.

"She'll kill you!" Kenny shouted and laughed – the crazed laugh of a man who was just about to step off a cliff face.

"Sure," I said, and fired a couple of defensive shots towards the door to cover my movements as I made my way back towards Kenny. I wasn't going to wait for her to make the next move. Somebody dropped in the hall; I didn't know if I'd hit anyone, not that I cared just now. I just wanted to buy some time. Kenny's eyes widened as I pointed the gun in my left hand against his forehead and barked, "Get up or I'll blow your brains out!" I fired another shot through the opening to show that I meant business. Kenny looked at me, but didn't move, so I hit him on the forehead with the gun barrel and fired another shot. He screamed and fell back to the floor.

"Get up!" I hissed.

"You won't get away, Hugo," D. S. Muller shouted from the hall.

"We'll see about that," I shouted back, firing another shot. The sound of my gunshots reverberated in my ears, but I ignored the discomfort.

Kenny got up – he believed my threat. "What now Hugo? Killing me won't help you. She'll kill you anyway," he groaned as he swayed unsteadily.

"Move back!" I ordered, as I edged towards the large bay window, my left-hand gun to the back of Kenny's neck, using him as a human shield, with the other gun aimed at the opening. A quick glance confirmed Sheila was on the floor, white as a ghost with terror in her eyes. Deciding she constituted no threat, I quickly brought my focus back.

The fact that D. S. Muller hadn't fired into the room told me she would only do so when she had a clear view. Maybe she'd change her mind, but I wasn't hanging around to see if that happened. At the window, I poked the gun deep into Kenny's fleshy neck, told him to stop, and fired another shot through the opening. I was running out of ammunition for that weapon, but I hadn't used the other one yet. In a rapid sequence, I pulled the blinds down, kicked Kenny back into the room, and fired two more shots past him. Dropping the gun into my jacket pocket, I grabbed a small but solid table, lifted it with my free hand and flung it through the large window, breaking the glass. I fired another shot, threw myself through the opening, landed on my shoulder on the grass and rolled onto my feet. I ran towards the wall, dropped the remaining gun in my pocket, and scrambled over, as a couple of shots hit next to me. I had speed, agility and technique, and maybe even the gods on my side.

Back on the street, I felt my heart racing, but I was in complete control. My senses were sharp and tuned; I was still in combat mode. I quickly scanned my surroundings. The street was pretty much deserted – a couple of bikes lay abandoned – the mayhem had scared everybody away. I could hear multiple sirens approaching, and knew I needed to get away. If the police caught me here, then I would be behind bars for a considerable time. There were still matters to be resolved before that could happen.

I started running in the opposite direction from where I'd come, and from where the sirens were coming. I crossed the street and ran down the drive of a house with a generous garden, taking only a few seconds to pass through the gate and run across the back garden. I didn't know where I was running to, I just needed to get as far away as possible. Charlie was a big boy and could handle himself.

Another fence navigated, landing me in the back garden of what appeared to be an empty house, where I stopped and leaned up against the side wall – in the shadows, getting my breath back. I could hear a cacophony of sirens, and they were multiplying. I was still too close. A quick check confirmed no injuries. I pushed away from the wall and walked to the front of the house.

People were venturing back out into the street, looking anxious, unsure about what was going on. Inquisitive kids were being ushered back inside, as the ripple of mayhem was spreading like waves from an epicentre. I needed to get away quicker than the speed my feet could manage. A car had stopped in the street – a Golf, the owner had got out and was talking to an older guy on the pavement. The engine was still running: that was my chance – right there! I took the black ski mask out of my pocket and put it over my head; it covered my face, with slots for my eyes and mouth. Bringing out my gun, I ran out towards the car. The guy on the pavement saw me first – an older gentleman with white hair. Maybe he was a combat veteran because he didn't freak out, but simply laid a hand on the guy he was talking to and pulled him away from the car. I guess he read my intention and just wanted to make sure his friend didn't get shot trying to be a hero. I didn't say anything, just ignored the screams around me as I slotted myself into the car, flipped the gear lever into first and floored the accelerator.

I knew I didn't have long before my stunt was reported, and this car would be red hot. I drove around a corner, slowed down, removed the ski mask and hoped nobody would pay attention to just another car driving down the street. A couple of minutes later I came to a junction and continued through. A woodland appeared on my right, so I swung into a car park, parking as far away from the road as I could. A couple of other cars were there too, but no one was to be seen. I got out and carefully looked around, listening for anything untoward. A siren was approaching, and I cursed as I ran into the woods and hid behind a tree. A police car, a big SUV, the type used by armed response, screamed down the road. It was driving towards the direction I'd come from, so I gathered the police still were working to establish control. But I was pretty sure the man in the black ski-mask who'd taken the Golf would be hunted, and imminently so. Then I heard a helicopter coming in from the east: it was a police helicopter. With the cover of trees, I began running away from the car park. Nobody was around so far – I scanned my surroundings as I ran. The further away I could get without being seen, the better. But my time here in the woods was also limited; there would be dogs, and they had the scent from the car to follow.

It didn't take long before the woodland path emerged onto a road. Edinburgh was ahead of me, so I decided to head back into the city and hide in the urban jungle while searching for Julia. I needed to see her face-to-face, this was now personal to me.

The thought that Ariella might be dead suddenly hit me. Even though she had sold me out, I couldn't help but feel sad. Something about her had touched me deep inside. It wasn't just sexual attraction, but something deeper and more profound. I believed her to be a damaged individual, but with a good, if somewhat flawed heart, despite the facts to the contrary. The grief about her daughter had destroyed her from within.

"At least you're with Chloe now," I whispered to myself as I pulled the collar up on my jacket and ventured down the road. I remembered something Emily told me, something she had said to friends and teachers, "Dad believes in Heaven, but not in God."

She had a point. The sudden thought of Emily was sore. I felt an urgent need to call her, but I knew I couldn't. A call from me now would only cause her more distress and generate questions I couldn't answer.

Suddenly, the sound of a car approaching grabbed my attention; it was travelling fast and would be upon me within seconds.

TWENTY

I turned as the approaching car came to a screeching halt. To my relief I saw it was Charlie. He gestured for me to get in, not waiting for me to fasten my seatbelt before driving off, his face hard and focused on the road.

"Lucky for you I was coming this way, Hugo. What the blazes happened?"

"Mayhem!" I replied and let out a sigh of relief. I couldn't believe my luck; my nine lives surely must've been used up by now.

"Indeed. You know you can't run from this, don't you?"

"Yes, I know, but I still have some business to finish before I turn myself in," I said, and fished out my mobile, collecting my thoughts for a moment before I swiped the screen and made the call.

Charlie decided against saying anything else, and just focussed on the driving. He was heading back to the city centre, which was fine with me. I sensed he was about to bail out – fair enough – this whole thing had become worse than a mess, it was now a confirmed disaster. A ride back into the city centre was good enough for me, Charlie had helped me more than enough.

Petite's voice on the other end of the line summoned both our attention. "Hugo, you okay?"

There was obvious concern in her voice. I guessed she'd been listening to police radio frequencies and was aware of the drama that had unfolded. She had access to that sort of technology, which was what I needed right now.

"Yes, I'm okay. A lot has happened, as I guess you know. I'm on the run, Petite, and time's fast disappearing – I need you to guide me here."

"Right, you got it, Hugo!" That was my Petite, not a second of hesitation.

"Cool, first, anything on the police radio about me?" I asked.

"Yes, you're a wanted man! The police believe you're the individual who escaped from a major crime incident scene. Was that you, Hugo?" Petite asked. I assumed she was encrypting this call, otherwise she would have warned me not to say too much.

"Yes, I was there, so was Kenny Bullard, Mike, Sheila, Ariella and D. S. Rachel Muller, as well as a couple of thugs. It turned into a bloodbath, Petite. Tell me what you've heard on the radio." I glanced over at Charlie, who was listening intently, and nodded as I pointed at a turn-off coming up. I needed to hear this, and by the look on Charlie's face, so did he. He checked his mirrors and indicated to turn.

"My ... where shall I start ... the radio's gone mad, Hugo. The police were first called to a suspected domestic incident, which very quickly escalated to a suspected firearms incident. Then actual gun fire was reported, and this became a major ongoing crime incident. The first police units on the scene reported taking fire and had to retreat to await armed-response back up. Who is shooting at the police, Hugo?"

"D. S. Muller! She's a killer cop. Maybe she's decided to commit a shoot-out suicide, or something mental like that?" I rubbed my knuckles anxiously. Why would she do that? I didn't know, but as crazy as it sounded, it made sense. The woman I'd encountered was definitely unhinged. My own brother had been a cop who'd made a deal with the devil in a moment of weakness and greed. Then it was just a matter of an ever-more slippery slope, during which he'd committed some vicious crimes. It was a lesson learned: just carrying a cop I.D. card, didn't mean one couldn't end up in a very dark place.

"Petite, D. S. Muller is the one who killed both Jens and Cameron Bullard! Kenny had himself a cop assassin in his pay." As I spoke, the pieces of the puzzle were falling into place.

"That's crazy!" Petite said with genuine shock in her voice.

I looked over at Charlie, who by now had parked in a quiet side street and was sitting tapping his knee as he listened in. He was giving me time to figure out my next move. I was grateful for that.

"Why would Kenny have Jens Brekken killed?" Petite asked.

"He had a play going to finally kick his dad off the throne, so to speak. That poker game was to be the catalyst. I'm not sure if he intended Jens to be killed, or if the circumstances just got out of hand. But I'm convinced he was behind Cameron's murder, again maybe not in the sequence he'd originally planned, but this is total mayhem, Petite."

"Mayhem's the right definition, Hugo. The airwaves are full of police activity now, just hold for a minute …"

I leaned back in the seat and closed my eyes for a moment. Had I hit anybody as I fired? I hoped not, a murder charge would mean serious time, even if I claimed self-defence. The guns were still on me. They needed to disappear. I turned to Charlie, who was looking at me, equally deep in thought.

"Charlie, I've got both guns. And I fired one several times."

"Both guns?" Charlie gave me hard stare as he tried to process that information.

"Yes, I took one from Mike. I need to get rid of them."

"You certainly do! Let's get rid of them now," Charlie said, as he put the car into drive and pulled away.

I was about to reply, when Petite's adrenaline-charged voice came back on the mobile.

"The police are about to bring the situation under control. The shooter – guess that's D. S. Muller – is believed to be dead, apparently killed as armed officers encircled the house. Armed response is moving in … hang on …"

I could hear radio chatter in the background but couldn't make any sense of it. Petite was listening intently; her breathing was heavy with excitement. I waited – this was real time. Charlie was listening too, whilst driving east through the southern part of Edinburgh. I wasn't sure where he was heading, but I guessed it was towards somewhere I could get rid of the weapons. He wasn't bailing just yet, something I was grateful for. I'd be in his debt for a long time to come.

"Right, reports of multiple casualties ..." Petite paused again, she was relaying the information as she received it. It felt surreal listening to the stream of events, considering that I'd been there myself, just under an hour ago.

"They've found three alive: two males ... a female – not D. S. Muller – another female, found inside, presumed dead ... who might that be?" Petite asked absently, as she paused to listen to the reports.

I knew the dead female had to be Ariella. I shook my head, how tragic that her life had ended like this, killed after being caught up in a spiralling mess that I doubted she'd fully signed up to. My gut instinct told me Ariella had been played by Julia and had paid the ultimate price.

"You okay there, Hugo?"

Charlie's question brought my focus back. I looked at him and nodded, then re-focused on the call where the radio chatter was still going at full throttle in the background.

Petite came back, "All right, armed response have secured the premises ... paramedics are now allowed in. The two males are injured. Okay. A female is in shock but not injured. Another male is presumed dead, head trauma ... and ... hold on, Hugo ..."

I held my breath, what had happened to Kenny? The thought of him somehow having managed to escape made my anger blaze to a thousand degrees. And if he had, then this was by no means over.

"Hugo, you said Kenny was there?"

"Yes, he was there." I paused, realising this wasn't over. Kenny had escaped.

"Petite, I obviously don't know for sure, but I bet he's not one of the two injured guys. There were two thugs there, one of them was Gary, who I thought was working for Ariella. Unless, the police find him hiding in the house somewhere, it looks like Kenny's got away." In my peripheral vision, I noticed Charlie raising an eyebrow. I put Petite on pause, and looked over at him.

"Charlie, I need to keep the guns," I said in a tone not inviting debate.

Charlie nodded and looked back at me. "I hear you, Hugo. Don't take this the wrong way, but do you think going after Kenny is a viable option?"

"Maybe not, but still, I don't think I have a choice. The scumbag was going to frame me with murder. The man's a monster, and he won't ever leave me, or any of my loved ones, in peace. I need to get to him before he gets to those I love. This was personal to him, he told me so to my face, now this is personal to me, Charlie."

I stared through the front windscreen of the Jaguar. Charlie didn't reply; he knew by the tone of my voice I'd made my mind up. I didn't know how I was going to do this, but I knew I had to. My family and I were on Kenny's hit list, I needed to make sure that list was obliterated.

A steel grey sky had encompassed the city of Edinburgh; rain was coming again. It felt fitting, right even, that a certain darkness had descended on us.

"Okay, Hugo, but first you need to clean up, and we need to get off the road. I've got a property – not registered to my name – in Musselburgh. It has a garage with another car there that you can use. What do you say?"

"Sounds good to me, let's go," I said.

"Good," Charlie replied, and nodded towards the phone in my hand. "Petite still on the line, Hugo?"

"Thanks, Charlie," I said as I activated Petite's line. "You still there, Petite?"

"Yes,"

"Anything else, any mention of Kenny?"

"Nothing about Kenny. The inventory so far is two males injured, one female apparently okay and two others – a male and a female – found dead, all five inside the house. D. S. Muller was shot outside the house. Apparently, she came charging out with her gun blazing. One of the police snipers took her out. Deliberate suicide by a police bullet, according to the officers who were present. They're all pretty shocked, it was like nothing any of them had ever experienced." Petite paused, then continued, "What's your plan now, Hugo?"

"That's still to be worked out, Petite. You good to keep going? You safe?"

"Yes, I'm home, Hugo. My flat is like a fortress, don't worry about me. But there is another thing I need to mention."

"What's that, Petite?"

"Jimmy called – he needs to talk to you. I got a number for you."

TWENTY-ONE

"Hello," Jimmy said cautiously, as he answered my call.

"Jimmy, it's Hugo." I paused; I wanted to hear what he had to say before I continued. I didn't trust him just now.

"Hugo! Where are you?" Jimmy asked in a serious tone.

I took a moment, reminding myself that Jimmy was a master manipulator. That was his greatest asset as a defence lawyer, playing those around him to ensure he achieved the desired outcome. He'd told me this himself. Now I couldn't help but wonder if he was playing me?

"I'm out and about, where are you?" I replied. A silence fell between us, as both waited for the other to show his hand first. I shook my head as anger ignited deep within. Jimmy was my friend, or so I had believed. Not that friendship seemed to matter any longer. I quelled the growing anger within and continued to wait. It was up to Jimmy now. If this conversation ended here and now, then so be it.

"I'm with somebody you've been looking for," Jimmy finally said.

I clenched my left fist and shook it. Charlie looked at me, he'd noticed my silent gesture of frustration. "Right, Jimmy, who?" The adrenaline was rapidly racing inside me, but I kept my voice steady and calm. If Jimmy was with Julia, then she was finally reaching out. If he wasn't, maybe he was setting up a trap for me on behalf of Kenny Bullard.

"You don't trust me, Hugo, do you?" Jimmy stated in a matter-of-fact manner. No guilt or remorse was detectable in his voice. A sad state of affairs for sure, but it was what it was.

"Can I? Would you?" I asked, just stopping myself from launching into a rant. That would've achieved nothing, and my goal to get out of this mess in one piece, with no nasty surprises waiting down the line for my family, or myself.

"Fair enough, Hugo," Jimmy paused, putting his phone on hold. He was talking to somebody else. Was that Julia Felt?

Next to me, Charlie cleared his throat to attract my attention. Without taking his eyes away from the road, he asked, "What's going on, Hugo?"

"It's Jimmy, and I think he's with Julia. I don't know what they want to achieve here."

Charlie shot me a sharp look, but I made a quick gesture for him to stay silent as Jimmy's voice came back on the line.

"Hugo, the person I'm with wants to meet with you. Tonight."

"Who is it, Jimmy? Who wants to meet with me?" I asked calmly.

There was a silence before Jimmy replied, "I can't say, but it's somebody you definitely want to meet." He paused and waited.

"Right ... okay then, let's make it a time and a place of my choosing. You guys know what's happening here. If you and the person you're with want to get out of this mess in one piece, you'd better agree."

"Is that a threat, Hugo?" Jimmy's voice now had a sharpness tinged by anger. He was like me: a guy who didn't respond well to ultimatums. But now it was time for him to be presented with one.

"You bet, Jimmy. Take it or leave it. Just so you know, Kenny Bullard's back – he's ended his old man and is running amok. Do you guys want to run forever?"

I was hoping to rattle Jimmy, unless of course he was working for Kenny in the first place. In fact, I now couldn't rule that out; at the moment, I couldn't rule anything out. Jimmy's breathing on the other end of the line appeared to shift up a notch. I assumed both Julia and Jimmy would know Kenny was back, but maybe not that Cameron had been killed. The police had been lucky so far: there had been no news leak, and Cameron Bullard's murder was still a secret.

"Hugo, listen, I know you don't trust me just now, and who can blame you? But we're on the same side here! Call me on this number when you've got some instructions for us – I won't be available for the next hour though. And tell Petite to keep her doors locked!"

Jimmy terminated the call before I could reply. Petite – was she now a target? It dawned on me, she would be. The reality behind that thought sent shivers down my spine. With or without help from Jimmy and Julia, it made sense for Kenny to get hold of Petite.

"Damn." I said loudly.

"What's up?" Charlie asked as he swung the car into the drive of a neat, detached bungalow. I ignored the question and quickly rang Petite's number, but this time she didn't answer. It seemed to ring forever, before switching to her voice mail. I left a quick message, terminated the call, and immediately rang again, but again it went unanswered.

"Kenny will go after Petite. I gotta warn her," I looked over at Charlie, I hadn't considered that possibility until now. Feeling a dread forming like a heavy, growing lump in my stomach, I silently cursed myself.

"He will. You're right," Charlie spoke quietly as he reached for his phone to access his garage port app and open the double garage ahead. Then he eased the car in, just as I ended my third unsuccessful call to Petite. Where was she? I just spoke to her not long ago. I got out of the Jaguar, which Charlie had parked next to a big Mercedes SUV, black with dark-tinted rear windows.

"Jump in the back, Hugo. Lie low. Let's go and see if we can get Petite."

Charlie slotted himself behind the wheel, while I eased into the back and sat low in the seat. The tinted rear windows were so dark, it was next to impossible to see inside. I looked at Charlie as he backed the SUV down the drive, and felt a glow of appreciation. He wasn't bailing out any time soon, and I owed him big time.

"Thanks Charlie," I said quietly, catching his eye in the rear-view mirror.

"I'm not just doing this for you, Hugo. I like Petite – and besides, Peter Williams would never forgive me if I let anything heinous happen to his one-and-only child!"

I didn't reply, just nodded, reminded of the fact that Charlie and Peter knew each other well; they'd done business together and their families had socialised together for decades. Peter had been out of the game for years, but he and Charlie shared a lot of history. They were friends, and Charlie never would let a friend down.

I gazed out of the window as Charlie headed towards Morningside, where Petite's flat was. A cloud cover had settled above the city of Edinburgh, mirroring the gloom of my mood. I couldn't let anything bad happen to Petite! Although she was more than capable of looking after herself, nevertheless I felt responsible for her safety.

"It could be a trap, Charlie. I don't trust Jimmy just now," I said, picking up the sound of an emergency siren somewhere in the distance.

"That's true, Hugo, but we gotta get hold of her, nonetheless. Get back on that phone, Hugo, and call her." Charlie paused, then added, "I thought she had the mobile more or less surgically implanted, no?"

Under different circumstances, his comment would've been amusing, but I didn't laugh, and neither did Charlie. The situation was not funny. Petite was glued to her phone most of the day, but when my call again went onto voice mail, it became apparent that the glue had become unstuck.

I cursed, staring at my phone screen. Maybe I should try and get hold of somebody close to her, somebody who could nip over to see if she was okay. I knew one of her close girlfriends lived in the same building, two storeys down if I remembered correctly. I was about to make a call when suddenly blue lights flashed behind us, penetrating the tinted rear window and pulsating through the SUV.

TWENTY-TWO

"Stay calm," Charlie mumbled as he checked his wing mirror, then indicated and steered the SUV towards the kerb. I slumped lower in the seat, sank down out of sight and eased myself towards the kerb-side door. The blue lights behind us continued to pulse through the cabin for what felt like an eternity.

"I'm gonna do a runner, Charlie," I said, laying my hand on the door handle. getting ready to bolt.

"Wait." Charlie spoke sharply, whilst keeping his focus on the mirror.

I waited, tensed up, ready to go. Then the police car behind started to overtake, coming to a sudden stop beside us. The sirens were now on full throttle, warning a drunk guy to get out of the way, but it seemed he wasn't for moving. He was a typical drunk, standing in the path of the police car, in the middle of the road, more than ready for an argument or a fight if things went that way. The guy stood swaying from side to side, but didn't move out of the way as he gestured provocatively towards the police. I felt like getting out myself and dragging the fool away so that the police car could move on: I wanted it gone.

"Idiot!" Charlie hissed, and slapped the wheel.

The passenger copper got out and tried to move the guy off the road. The drunk took a clumsy swing at him, but the copper easily evaded the ungainly blow, grabbed hold of the fool, pushed him hard and sent him flying out of the way. The coppers were obviously in a hurry, as the police car pulled forward to let its passenger back in and then took off at full throttle.

"If that had happened in Jamaica, the police would've just run the idiot over, or simply shot the fool ... You guys don't know you're born!"

Charlie's disgust was obvious as he flipped the gear lever into drive. He'd just released the brakes when the fool stumbled back into the road, flipping rude gestures and shouting after the long-gone police car. Charlie slammed the brakes back on, shouted an impressive range of expletives at him, then hit the horn. The drunk guy turned towards us – again, he wasn't for moving.

I'd had enough! "Just a minute," I said to Charlie, and got out. I quickly approached the drunk, who was now facing our vehicle, blood streaming from a deep laceration on top of his nose. He turned towards me and broke a bloody grin, his face covered in blood, his hair standing upright with vomit, and the front of his shirt equally contaminated.

"Right Mister, you want a thrashing?" slurred the guy, before launching into a hoarse laugh. He was the stereotypical 'Braveheart' wannabe – fuelled stupid on booze. I didn't reply; talking to drunks is a waste of time. I easily dodged his uncoordinated swing and quickly moved to his side. Not wishing to soil my hands by touching the guy, I kicked him hard to his hip, sending him flying again, and out of the way of our vehicle. I jumped back into the car and Charlie took off, shaking his head in disbelief.

"I bet that guy will be picked up by an ambulance and taken to hospital, where he'll cause mayhem for the next few hours before he falls asleep in a comfortable bed!"

"Yup, and no matter what mess he makes of himself, he'll be cleaned up by the nursing staff, and then when he's sober enough and the doctors have checked him over – free of charge – he'll be sent home. Compliments of the tax payer." I replied, also shaking my head in disgust. All this expense for an adult idiot who couldn't handle his alcohol.

"Wrong. It's just wrong," Charlie mumbled as he drove on.

"Definitely," I agreed, and rang Petite again, but once more the call went to voicemail. I slapped my thigh in frustration and caught Charlie's glance in the rear-view mirror.

"We'll be there in less than five minutes, Hugo."

"Drop me off at the top of the street. Find good parking, Charlie, where you can quickly reach the front door of Petite's apartment building. You got charge on your phone?"

"Yes, you call me, Hugo. Oh, and leave me one of the guns. If you need a hand up there, you don't hesitate to call, okay? Petite is special, she's off limits, everybody knows that! Kenny should know that – if he doesn't, then he'll have to pay. I may not be a young buck any more, but I can still handle myself."

I nodded, my lips tightly closed together, a nervous charge ramming through my veins. Charlie was right: Petite was off limits, and everybody knew that – Cameron Bullard had known that, when he was calling the shots. For all that he was, or more precise; had been, Cameron Bullard had a code. Kenny hadn't, as was a common trait amongst the nastier examples of inheritance-gangster types. I quickly got the guns out, checked them both, and dropped the one for Charlie into the deep storage box between the front seats.

Arriving at Petite's street, Charlie brought the SUV to a halt at the top of the street and I stepped out. Charlie and I gave each other a knowing look before he drove off. I would call if I needed to, but I hoped it wouldn't come to that. If I had to call Charlie, then things must've really gone pear-shaped. I looked down the street, cars parked all along it, street lights casting cylinders of light in a dark, foggy environment. The evening was miserable, the moisture thick in the air, giving promise of a cold, wet night. I didn't care, if anything the twilight was good for me, providing decent cover outside the light circles of the street lamps. I ventured down the street, scanning the area around me. Petite's apartment was on the top floor. If I kept close to the building, anybody looking down would have great difficulty making out who I was, which would be handy if Kenny was waiting up there for me. I tried Petite's mobile again, but once more I was connected to voice mail.

Outside the building I took another sweep of the surroundings, I didn't recognise any of the cars parked by the kerb. Nobody standing across the street, nobody to be seen. Just a miserable Edinburgh evening. I took a deep breath, opened my leather jacket so I could easily reach my gun and stepped up to the front door. Normally it would be locked, but now it was open; whoever had used it last hadn't closed it properly. I pushed the door open and looked into the concrete hallway. A couple of white lights gave the interior a cold feeling. In the back, a bike was partially blocking the passageway to the rear courtyard. I stepped in, looked up the staircase and stopped. I took a moment to listen. A low murmur of vague noise descended from above, music and TV, somebody laughing loudly, maybe somebody having an argument, just normal life as far as I could hear.

Suddenly the ground-floor apartment door to my right opened. I swung around, reached inside my jacket and grabbed my gun. A young couple came out, but stopped dead when they saw me. The guy stepped forward, putting himself between his female companion and me.

"You okay mate?"

There was fear in the guy's voice and he lowered his eyes as he saw my arm disappearing under my jacket. Looking at him, I was sure he wasn't the kind to know about guns. Still, one only needed to watch TV and have a little imagination to speculate about what I was concealing under my jacket. It didn't help that I looked the part. He looked up, and now fear was more evident in his eyes. His female companion started to retreat into the flat.

"Yes, no worries, mate. You guys just startled me, that's all."

I laughed; it sounded genuine enough for the young couple to relax just a little, and for the female to stop retreating. I let go of my gun, pulled my hand out, gave them a big smile and turned to walk up the stairs. I was aware of them watching me, unsure about what they'd seen, unsure about what to do next. I kept walking up the stairs. Then they decided, closed their front door, made sure it was locked and hurried out. I cursed under my breath as I looked back. If anything happened here, one thing was for sure, they would remember me clearly and would be able to give the police a full description. That's life, one could never account for circumstances.

I silently hurried to the top landing and stopped at Petite's front door. Taking a moment to listen didn't reveal anything, there was no noise to be heard from the flat. I eased close to Petite's front door and made sure I couldn't be seen through the peep-hole. The door was shut and looked normal, nothing to indicate it'd been forced open. I glanced over at the other doors and calmly pulled out my gun, shielding it in front of me so if anybody was watching, it couldn't be seen. I knew Petite's door was solid with a very substantial lock, but I had a key. I didn't ring the bell, but with my free hand got the key out and with as little noise as possible slotted it into the hole. The click sounded awfully loud, but nothing happened. I positioned myself up against the wall and opened the door. It swung open without much noise, the hinges well oiled. Again nothing. With my gun poised and ready, I peeked around into the flat. It was dark inside, only the light from the corridor illuminating the hallway. I felt my heart rate hike up a notch as I stepped inside and closed the door behind me. I waited for my vision to adjust to the darkness. A sweet-scented aroma hung in the air, Petite loved her natural scents.

With my gun aimed I checked the flat, until I was satisfied there was nobody there. I kept the lights off and used my small but powerful torch to examine the rooms again, looking for clues to where she was. Nothing – her workstation neat, tidy and all shut down; I knew there wasn't any point in trying to gain access to Petite's computers – she had several – they would all be better protected than most countries' intelligence services.

"Where are you, Petite?" I asked myself as I looked around. I tried her phone again, it didn't ring this time, just went straight to voicemail. I left another message, "Petite, its Hugo, please call me. I'm worried about you!"

Then I called Charlie.

"Hugo, what's happening?"

"I'm in her flat, but she isn't here," I said as I sat down at her workstation.

"Right, anything – any clue as to where she might be, or what's happened?"

Charlie's voice was intense and full of stress. I hadn't realised he felt this way about Petite. Charlie wasn't the type to be stressed; if anything, stressful situations made him calmer and more focused.

"Nothing, no signs of a struggle, nor break in for that matter." I looked around again; there was nothing on her desk other than her 3 screens, a keyboard and a mouse. I tried the drawers, but they were all locked. That was maybe a little paranoid, but it was very much in line with the Petite I knew. "Things look normal. Just as if she left in a normal fashion," I said, tapping the desk with my fingers, in frustration.

"Maybe she did, Hugo," Charlie paused for a moment, "Right, meet me back on the street. You need to get out of there. The police might arrive at any time."

I looked around, the darkness felt comforting. Some people were uncomfortable in darkness, even so-called tough guys. Not me, I always found it somehow reassuring: the darkness was my friend, always had been, always would be. I moved up to the window and looked out on the steel grey sky above; it was like a lid on the city below. Standing in the darkness of the flat looking out at a world where the colours had been drained off, I felt a strange sense of peace. And I felt alone …

"What am I doing?" I whispered to myself. The question itself surprised me as much as my being the one to ask it. I didn't have an answer. Something caught my eye on the street below. A couple of lights appeared, car lights cutting through the twilight. Suddenly they disappeared – turned off – but I was pretty sure the car was still there on the street, not parked, just idling, waiting to spring into action at any moment.

TWENTY-THREE

It wasn't the police, it was Kenny. As adrenaline-fuelled energy raced through my veins, I felt stoked for whatever was to come. I needed to unleash that energy, but I was finished running. Looking out of the window, I calmly checked my weapon: the clip was full and the gun was working. I dropped it into my leather jacket pocket for now and cracked my knuckles – it was a habit of mine. I thought I could see a couple of shadows passing over the circular spots of light from the street lamps. I checked my phone and debated with myself as to why Charlie hadn't called. Now the questions had to be asked: was Charlie in with Kenny? Was Petite in with Kenny? Could I trust anybody? Just now I decided I couldn't. I checked my phone again and made sure it was on silent and with the vibrate function off too.

I quickly went to the front door of the flat and stopped to listen; there was no noise detectable from the corridor outside and nobody to be seen through the peep hole. Unless they were there already, up against the walls either side, waiting? That was a gamble I had to take, I wasn't going to wait in the flat, like a sitting duck. I brought my gun out again and grabbed hold of the handle. I hadn't locked the door in case I had to make a hasty retreat. I took a breath and then rapidly swung it open. Nobody there. I scanned the corridor – nothing – then I calmly exited the flat, and carefully closed and locked the door. Down the corridor there was a shared room with a waste-disposal unit and some other domestic appliances for the flats on this floor. I'd used it a couple of times in the past, helping Petite to tidy up after dinner parties and such. Moving over towards the staircase I heard somebody enter the building down below. It could be a resident, or could be Kenny; time would tell.

Moving quickly, I let myself into the domestic room, leaving the door ajar, so that I still had a decent view of Petite's door. I noticed a black, nondescript box above the door, and decided it was a camera, which I'd never noticed before. It had to be Petite's doing. This presented more questions: had I been watched as I entered and hid here in this domestic cupboard? If so, who was watching?

It was too late to do anything about that as I heard footsteps coming up the staircase. I rolled my shoulders, loosened up and got ready to explode into action. Then I waited and listened.

A man came into sight, stopped and took his time looking up and down the corridor. As he looked towards the domestic room, my mouth went dry. It was Jimmy Johnson. He was wearing a dark suit, with a black coat and black gloves. Although elegantly dressed, he looked rough. I held my breath as he stepped towards Petite's door and stopped to listen. A moment of silence, as we both waited.

"You there, Hugo?" Jimmy called out calmly, without looking in my direction.

I pushed the door open, my gun aimed at him. "What the blazes are you doing here, Jimmy?" I asked, stepping into view.

Jimmy turned and looked at me, his eyes widened as he saw my gun. "Calm down, Hugo, and put that piece away!" He raised his hands and said, "We need to talk, but not here."

We sure did need to talk, and Jimmy was right about one thing: this was not the place to have that conversation. A resident might appear at any time, so standing here with a gun was not a good idea. But trusting Jimmy, here and now, was equally problematic.

"You here alone?" I asked, not sure if I would trust him whatever he claimed.

Jimmy nodded, and spoke with an intense urgency in his voice, "Yes, now put that piece away. Listen, I know Petite's not here, and I know you have a key. Let's go inside and talk." He kept his eyes on me.

I listened intently but couldn't detect anybody else waiting to ambush me. Another decision to make. He sounded genuine, so I decided to go with him, another throw of the dice – it had to be done. I put the gun in my pocket but kept my hand on it, stepped fully into the corridor and checked the staircase – nobody there. I extracted the key from my pocket with my free hand and offered it to Jimmy. His eyes narrowed as he took it from me and then turned to unlock the door.

"You first, Jimmy, put the light on and walk in. I need you to walk inside, away from the door, then stand with your hands visible," I said in a low voice. I wanted to make sure there would be enough room for me to follow him inside and close the door behind us, without my being too close to my captive.

Jimmy did as he was instructed, and I did a final check behind me – still nobody there – before I followed Jimmy inside. He kept his distance, which I needed him to do. I still had my pistol aimed at him and just now I wouldn't hesitate to use it. Jimmy wasn't a fool, he knew that.

"You don't trust me, Hugo, I know that, but let me explain," Jimmy said as he slowly turned to face me.

"Yeah, that's a really good idea," I replied as I locked the door.

"First of all, let me assure you that I'm here as your friend."

"Right, we'll see about that. First tell me; how you knew I was here?"

"Charlie told me …" Jimmy paused, looked at me for a moment before he continued, "he's fine, I've sent him home. He doesn't need any more involvement in this mess."

Jimmy's assertiveness was a little too strong for my liking just now, but then again, he'd always been like that, nothing new there.

"Charlie called you?" I asked.

"No, I called him, and Charlie decided to trust me."

"Why?"

"Because I told him I'd managed to convince Petite to get out of here. This is not a safe place, Hugo. Nowhere linked to you or Petite is safe just now."

"But why did you tell Petite to leave?"

Jimmy took a deep breath; I could tell he was getting frustrated, but so be it, I needed him to spell out what he knew, and his answers would tell me whether I could trust him or not. I also knew we were in an unsafe location, but that couldn't be helped just now either. We weren't moving until I was satisfied. I made a small hurry-up gesture for him to continue with his explanation.

"Because Kenny Bullard's on your tail and he wants you dead ... really, Hugo, weren't you just involved in that crazy shoot-out earlier? It's all over the news. Obviously, the police are looking for you too, but it's Kenny I'd worry about if I were you. And Kenny knows Petite is probably just about the only person you trust right now ...," Jimmy paused, fixed my eyes, then said, "And I care about Petite, Hugo. You know that."

"All right, now tell me, where's Julia? Was she with you?"

Jimmy nodded before replying, "Yes, she was, but not any more; after I'd talked to you she disappeared. Don't know why – something spooked her." Jimmy stopped and studied my reaction. He could tell that I didn't believe him. "Believe or not, Hugo, it's the truth. I thought she'd just gone to the bathroom, but she simply disappeared. Not like she was my prisoner ... I mean, she came to me." Jimmy stopped and raised his hands in frustration. "Listen, Hugo, it might sound daft, but I'm convinced I'm being played here, just how, I'm not sure, but Julia's surely done a number on me."

I took a breath, allowing myself to process what Jimmy had told me. Part of me didn't want to believe him, but it kind of made sense and certainly corresponded with what I knew so far. A thought suddenly popped up in my head. The little demon guy, who never trusted anybody and who resided in the depths of my consciousness, spoke up:

"Are you keeping me here until Kenny arrives?" I asked calmly. "If so, Jimmy, then I swear on my mother's grave I'll shoot you first."

Jimmy raised his hands again, this time in a gesture of surrender, his eyes widened again as he stared down the barrel of my pistol, pointed straight at his face. He was too far away to reach out and grab the gun or try any other move without my delivering a bullet straight through his face.

"No, no, calm down, Hugo! Listen to me, that's not the case. I'm your friend for Heaven's sake," Jimmy pleaded, with a faltering voice.

I couldn't remember Jimmy ever being afraid, but he was now. He wasn't a fool, and recognised the deadly intent in my eyes. So he should: I wouldn't hesitate to pull the trigger.

"Doesn't matter, Jimmy – friendship, when it comes down to it, is worth nothing to some types, and maybe you're one of those types? Maybe I've read you wrong for all these years?" My voice was hoarse and cold. I moved so that I wasn't standing in front of the door; it was a solid door, but a firearm would be able to penetrate it. Satisfied with my position for now, and with my gun still aimed at Jimmy's face, I spoke in a clear, even voice, "You need to tell me why I should believe you on this, Jimmy. And you need to be convincing. And you also need pray that Kenny doesn't arrive!"

"Right, right, Julia contacted me, just before I met you on Monday – told me she was involved in a difficult situation and would potentially need legal representation. She wouldn't disclose what it was, but pleaded with me to meet with her later to hear her out. I know Julia well, and like you and your brother, I like her … okay, I fancy her, always have! And I also knew her poker hadn't gone well in the last year, so she was running out of money. She pushed all the right buttons, and …" Jimmy stopped himself and looked down, shaking his head in frustration. If he was faking this, then he was a mighty actor.

"Damn my weakness," Jimmy finally said, and cursed as he looked back at me.

"What were you doing in her house, Jimmy," I asked.

Jimmy looked at me with surprise. "How do you know that?"

"Because I was there," I replied calmly. "Upstairs, listening to you and your crew getting all those paintings out – in a hurry too."

"Okay, Julia convinced me to empty her house of those paintings and take them to this warehouse. Said they were worth a fortune and would work as security towards my fee. Money talks, Hugo, you know that as well as I do, so being blinded by the almightiness of more cash, I did it." Jimmy stopped and looked at me, his face a little pale, his eyes drained of their usual confidence.

"Well, I guess those paintings could be worth a little money as art, but the real money comes when they're dissolved!" I spoke with a meaningful tone as I studied his reaction.

My gut instinct told me he hadn't previously known, but he now did. I told him my theory, which I believed to be fact: that the painting canvases were laced with cocaine and would dissolve, through the right chemical procedure, to produce pure high-quality cocaine. At the end of the process it would be ready to be mixed, cut and sold for millions. The Ariella Cantor Art Studio hadn't just been a renowned art dealership, but had also fronted an international drug-dealing empire. I'd suspected this for months, but something had stopped me from shopping her. Maybe it was my belief that she was a hostage to this set up; maybe it was my own guilt for not having found her missing daughter; maybe it was because of the deep-seated attraction I felt towards her; or maybe just because I felt deeply and profoundly sorry for her – I couldn't say for sure.

"I don't know what you're talking about, Hugo," Jimmy said with a still-faltering voice.

"Yes, you do, Jimmy."

"Drugs?" Jimmy replied after a painful moment.

"Yes indeed, millions' worth, and both Kenny and Julia are involved, although I must admit I hadn't realised that until very recently."

Jimmy looked away, his face flushed with anger. "Right, so what the blazes is actually going on here, Hugo?"

It was a very good question and the pieces were now starting to fall into place. I looked closely at Jimmy and decided to share my theories: theories I just knew were facts. I'd decided to believe him. For what it was worth, he was still a lawyer, and would be representing my brother in a trial that was beginning tomorrow – in just a few hours, in fact.

"Ultimately, if you ask me, it's Kenny cleaning house ...," I paused, letting that sink in. "Trust me, Jimmy, you don't want to be involved in this, regardless of what Julia might've told you. Where did you take the paintings?"

"To a warehouse down by Leith Docks, owned by a friend of Julia, a guy called Alan Trent. I checked him out, well I thought I did anyway, but obviously not thoroughly enough!" Jimmy looked up, angry with himself, before he continued, "Apparently a legitimate business man with a number of warehouses and a haulage business. Looked clean enough when I checked him out."

"Bet he did," I said, and laughed.

"I didn't look hard enough, Hugo." Jimmy's confidence snapped back and he pointed at my gun, "You want to put that away now, Hugo?"

"Maybe," I said – then there was a hard knock on the door.

TWENTY-FOUR

"Coppers," I whispered as I looked through the peep hole. I turned back quickly as I noticed Jimmy slowly approaching me; he displayed his hands as I trained the gun back on him.

"Listen, Hugo, let me deal with this," Jimmy whispered, calmly pushed my gun away and laid a hand on my shoulder. I allowed it to happen – we both knew there was no way I would shoot him. Still with the gun in my hand I gave him a hard look as the coppers outside knocked again, this time even harder.

"We don't have time here, Hugo, they'll bust through unless I open. It's a solid door, but they'll get through eventually. You want to start shooting coppers?" Jimmy whispered intensely as he leaned in. I shook my head.

"Good, listen now: you get out of sight and stay out of sight! If they don't have a search warrant, they won't get in; if they do, then I'll get you the best criminal defence there is in Scotland," Jimmy said, and gestured for me to get moving.

I did as the man said and moved quickly into Petite's bedroom, closing the door over. I kept the gun in my hand. Regardless of what happened I wouldn't drop the gun here and thus drop Petite in trouble. This was my gun, ergo my responsibility. I could see Jimmy through the crack of the door, getting himself ready to open to the police officers. There was no fire escape in Petite's apartment building, so the only way out was through the front door.

"Hello, how may I help you, officers?" Jimmy said a with strong voice, carrying the authority of a man who's used to being in charge.

"We're looking for Petite Williams," a Glaswegian voice replied. I looked on as Jimmy put his hands on his hips and kind of squared himself up, blocking the door, showing who was in charge. Classic Jimmy trade craft.

"She isn't here – is that all?" Jimmy paused, and I sensed something was wrong.

"Can I see your I.D. cards?" Jimmy asked with a hard tone, sensing the same. Something was definitely wrong. Then it clicked: they weren't real coppers.

"Here," a gruff voice said, and then I saw three big men, all dressed in police uniforms, push past Jimmy as they charged in through the door. Jimmy stumbled back, fighting hard to remain on his feet, cursing as he did. I didn't hesitate and ran out of the bedroom with the gun aimed.

"You clowns; keep your hands where I can see them," I shouted as I moved towards them. The guys stopped and looked at me in shock.

"Flamin' Hugo Storm!" The Glaswegian guy – the leader of the pack – sneered. I recognised him as one of Cameron Bullard's crew, well, now I guess he had a new boss.

"Kenny's looking for you," the big Glaswegian continued, glancing over at his mates.

I didn't fall for the trap, but kept my gun aimed at his face. "You really want to keep your hands visible, Shane ... You boys dress in cop uniforms now? Very creative!" I said.

As I spoke, Jimmy came in from behind Shane with a sturdy-looking vase. Shane saw it too late, and Jimmy smashed it over his head. The vase splintered, and Shane grunted a curse, took an unsteady step and then collapsed to the floor. The laceration sustained by the blow began to bleed. I redirected my aim at the other two goons, as I thought; what the hell Jimmy?

"You two, cover that wound – I don't want blood on my friend's floor – and pick that piece of garbage up, let's go!" I gestured with my gun in the face of one of the guys. He hesitated as he looked at his mate for direction. His mate recognised the determination in my face; he knew I wasn't messing about, so he nodded to his pal and they grabbed the unconscious Shane. He was a big guy and they struggled to drag him out of the flat. I followed, gesturing for them to continue down the stairs. Jimmy locked the door to Petite's flat as I followed the trio down the stairs, keeping my gun on the inside of my jacket. A number of residents came out onto the landings as we worked our way down, most of them curious about the noise. I flashed them my unofficial investigator card, which had the word 'POLICE' printed in bold.

"Police matter, please step back inside your flats, lock your doors and remain there until we tell you otherwise," I announced to all of them. It worked: they all hurried back into their flats, doors were slammed and locks turned.

"Neat," Jimmy said with appreciation in his voice.

We got down to the street, and Shane was still out cold. I checked his breathing, and found his airway was clear. The two other guys were out of breath after dragging their heavy pal down four flights of stairs. Jimmy then locked them all together around a lamp post with their own cuffs. I got a car key off one of them, a black bag from another and helped myself to Shane's mobile. My luck continued as his mobile wasn't secured by password, but by fingerprint, so I used Shane's thumb and unlocked his phone. Then I quickly changed the security settings from fingerprint to password access and entered a new one of my choosing. The other two goons started to curse both me and Jimmy, but we ignored them.

"The real police will be here soon, Hugo. What're you going to do?" Jimmy asked as he looked up and down the street.

"I'm going to get Kenny," I said as I looked at the car key.

"Okay, you be careful, you hear? Contact me when this is over and we'll arrange your orderly surrender to the police. And try not to kill anyone!" Jimmy offered his gloved hand.

"Don't worry about that. You focus on my brother's trial, Jimmy, and make sure Petite's okay. I'll find Julia, one way or another," I said as I shook his hand. It felt good to trust him again. I knew I wouldn't blame him, he'd made some bad moves but hadn't we all at times?

Jimmy flashed a wide grin. At the end of the day, he was an adrenaline junkie just like me.

We parted company, Jimmy turned and jogged over the street, disappearing through a narrow lane between the apartment buildings opposite. I looked at the cars parked along the kerb and saw a black BMW 5-series saloon. I ran up to it and pushed the unlock button on the key – it worked. Ignoring the shouts from the thugs locked around the lamp post, I got in, fired up the engine and pulled away from the kerb. As I drove onto the main road and away, I heard sirens in the distance.

I drove on, wanting to put some distance between myself and the drama behind. This car would soon be marked, but for now it would do. Traffic was non-existent at this hour and the fog was as thick as a Scottish tattie soup, low-lying and clinging to the stone buildings that lined the streets of Edinburgh, creating a mystic urban landscape around me. As the sirens faded into the background, I felt like I was the only one alive in this eerie urban landscape. My stomach rumbled as I tried to work out a plan. Nothing really presented itself. The mobile on the passenger seat beside me rang out – I picked it up.

"Shane, you got her yet?" Kenny's voice filled the cabin as I'd put it on loudspeaker.

"No, he hasn't," I replied.

Silence before Kenny came back on laughing, a truly vile and fake laugh that made me feel sick with disgust. "Well, if it isn't Hugo Storm! You really are doin' my head in now," Kenny hissed.

"You and me both, Kenny. Let's meet up and sort this, once and for all!"

I just wanted to get hold of this guy and literally squeeze the life out of him. I couldn't run much longer; the police would soon get to me, so I needed to get Kenny before that happened. Tam couldn't protect Claire and Emily forever, and Helena and the little ones down south wouldn't be safe either. Even with Helena's dad.

"Yeah, let's. Meet me down by the docks – Burton Street, Warehouse 15. I'll be waiting." Kenny terminated the call before I could reply.

I slowed down and stopped in a lay-by. Would it be a trap? Definitely. Would it be a mistake going there? Possibly. Would I do it anyway. Without a doubt. I took a breath of resolve and got Google Maps up on the phone. I was soon looking at street view; I recognised the place: it was the place where Douglas had killed a drug dealer six months ago. I leaned back and put my brain into overdrive: I could work with this, I would park a couple of streets away and approach on foot. Kenny wouldn't be alone, he'd have guys there; I had no illusions – they'd try to kill me for sure. But that was okay, because I'd kill them first. If I ended up in jail for a decade or two after this – I was looking at prison time anyway – it'd be worth it if it kept my family safe. I rolled my shoulders, closed my eyes and prepared myself mentally. Then I checked the street, flipped the gear lever into drive and floored the accelerator.

I arrived at my destination in twenty-five minutes, taking care to avoid the major roads through the city of Edinburgh, where the police would be trawling the streets. I parked the car and got out. The fog was lifting but it was still cold and miserable. I checked my gun and started walking towards the warehouse. My heart rate up just enough to provide me with the boost I needed so as to explode into action.; all my senses felt sharp and finely tuned. "Bring it on," I whispered to myself.

I approached the building from the south, climbed over a fence and squeezed through a narrow gap in another, stopping and listening at every corner before calmly moving on. I assumed Kenny would be running short on manpower, there couldn't be too many thugs left of the calibre he needed. Even so, I approached with care.

A cough from around a corner made me stop short. Then the person cleared his throat and spat and a vivid stream of cursing followed. The guy was fed up and so had become careless. That was his mistake. I tiptoed towards the corner and brought out a little mirror. The guy was now stomping his feet and making a lot of noise, which suited me just fine. I inched the mirror out low from my position and saw a guy, a big guy, lighting a cigarette. He was standing facing away from my corner. A quick scope showed nobody else around. I brought the mirror back, slipped it into my pocket and pulled out my gun. The guy was still stomping his feet, coughing and not paying much attention to his surroundings. Perfect. I wouldn't kill him if I could avoid it, but he definitely needed to be neutralised. I stepped out quickly and silently, reached out and grabbed the guy from behind, holding my gun to the back of his head.

"Don't make a sound or you die." I spoke with an intensity that told him I wasn't joking. He believed me, froze stock-still, with his hands out, the cigarette dangling from his lips.

"Step back with me," I instructed, as I pulled him back. He followed, stepping with leaden feet. Looking past him, I saw with relief that there didn't seem to be anybody watching. I guided him around the corner; he started to stumble as I pulled him harder. I sensed he was about to make his move, but he was too late. With my gun I hit him hard to the back of the head. He grunted and swayed, but remained on his feet, trying to fight back. I hit him again and this time the lights went out, his knees buckled and he collapsed to the ground. I took a minute to secure him with industrial-strength tape, procured from his colleagues, which I knew they'd planned to use on Petite.

I strode over the unconscious guy and peered around the corner. In front of me was the light-industrial unit, a workshop of some sort, where Kenny was waiting. I looked at the building and searched through my memory: six months ago I'd been brought here by my brother. Then as now, it looked abandoned, with just a single light above the entrance door and the garage port to its side closed and rusty. A narrow path disappeared on the right side of the building; I could try that, but I felt beyond it now. Looking at the building and feeling my burning fury inside, I knew I was about to toss caution to the wind and walk straight in. Come hell, or high water, I was going in.

Nobody came out to greet me as I walked quickly across the yard and nobody appeared from behind the junk and van wrecks dotted around. I rolled my shoulders again as I walked, loosening up and feeling energetic. But I knew this was me: walking straight into danger gave me a buzz like no other, my brother was the same, only even more extreme. I knew our dad had been like this, the stories I'd heard about him and the little I remembered confirmed it. That was just the way we Storm boys were wired, I guessed.

I entered through the front door with the barrel of my pistol following the aim of my torchlight. The inside was dark, dirty, with a faint mixed odour of oil and chemicals. I stepped into the foyer, it had been a reception area when this building had been in use. I stopped and listened – still nothing – just an eerie silence. In front were two doors, one leading into the workshop – a large space. I approached that door and swung it open, my torch cutting through the dusty darkness. I heard a muffled whine, which sounded like an animal. I stepped into the room whilst doing a three-sixty search with my torch. My gun followed the beam as I scanned my surroundings: there was junk everywhere, against all the walls. I took another step forward and was about to shout when I heard an excited voice urge, "Go, Buster, go and get him!"

I heard the unmistakeable growling of a dog, a big dog worked up into a frenzy and it was rushing towards me. I quickly found the black beast with the beam of my torchlight. I didn't have much time, five seconds and it would be on top of me. It was a big powerful dog, with a set of terrifying teeth and it was charging towards me. I like dogs, but not the kind that will rip my face off. As the beast howled and leaped towards me, I shot it and stepped aside. Dead instantly, the beast flew past me and crashed onto the dirty floor.

"Hey, Hugo," a familiar voice shouted to my right. I spun around to see Father Angus Black running towards me, his face covered in blood, his eyes wild and his clothes torn.

"What the ...," I shouted as I trained my weapon at him, only to realise another guy was coming fast towards me from my left, brandishing a baseball bat. I knew I'd made a mistake, I'd taken my last gamble and I'd lost. The baseball bat hit my head.

TWENTY-FIVE

As consciousness started to return, I became aware of a sound, muffled and distressed, slowly penetrating my stricken brain. I had a thumping headache that was squeezing my head tighter and tighter, almost beyond what I could tolerate. I continued to lie still, attempting to ascertain where I was. The left side of my face was in contact with a hard, cold, floor and dirt filled my nostrils and mouth as I lay on my left side. I was in a dark space, with a dank smell of chemicals hanging heavily in the air. My eyes were still shut, as I tried to get used to the headache. My breathing was controlled and I calmly fought the nausea that was coming in waves. I had sustained a head injury, but I also wanted to know if I all my extremities were intact. After a few minutes I concluded that they were. I could feel and move them all, albeit ever so slightly. The sound, a human sound, was now growing louder, as I discerned groans from a man in pain coming from my left. After listening for a little while, I thought I knew who it was. I allowed myself to open my eyes, slowly blinking as I did. Then I slightly moved my head, but a severe pain, like a knife being driven through my brain, cut through me, from ear to ear. I overrode it and took a deep breath. I was determined to try to sit up and get the lie of the land, head injury or not.

Suddenly, a bright light filled the space: naked white light from above coldly illuminated the area around me. I felt my head starting to spin and nausea exploding from within. I forced myself into a sitting position, but I couldn't contain the urge to vomit. Bile projected from my mouth, leaving behind its bitter taste and dizziness almost made me collapse, but somehow I managed to remain sitting upright.

"Messy," a hoarse voice shouted and laughed mockingly. Another two crude voices joined in with the laugher. I looked in their direction and recognised the man behind the voice: Kenny Bullard. He strode towards me, dressed in dark overalls, like a mechanic, and stopped directly in front of me, his eyes on fire with madness. "The Mighty Storm! Not so mighty now, eh? Feeling rubbish, son?" he taunted, grunting another laugh.

I fixed my eyes on him but didn't reply. The effort to remain sitting was just about all that I could manage at this point. Kenny continued to stare back at me, and I saw that there was more than just madness in his eyes, there was hatred too, raw pulsing hatred.

"Anyway, this is it for you, Hugo, this is the end of the line. You've caused me enough trouble as it is." Kenny's tone was flat and very matter-of-fact.

He focused his attention on the person to my left. I followed his gaze and saw that my earlier guess had been right: sitting on a solid wooden chair, tied down, head dropped forward, badly beaten, was Father Angus Black. He was barely conscious, whimpering in pain. Seeing him in such a state sent shivers running down my spine; was I next?

"This is the end of the line for Angus too, he's also out-lived his purpose. The idiot thought he could play me. Idiot!"

Kenny hissed, and gestured for his two tough-guy thugs to approach Angus. A pair of big dead-eyed brutes were also dressed in dark overalls, similar to Kenny. As they walked purposefully towards Angus, I noticed one of them had a knife – a big blade. I saw a grin growing on Kenny's face as the knife guy shot him a glance. Kenny hesitated for moment, then nodded. The guy with the knife slashed Angus across his face, jerking him back to consciousness as screams of pain and fear streamed from his bloodied mouth. Kenny walked over and slapped Angus with a gloved hand.

"Idiot," Kenny mumbled as he inspected the almost-surgical slash with disgust. Then he wiped the wound, with feigned care, on a rag supplied by the other thug, the one without the knife.

My head was now spinning at a slightly lower velocity and I was getting myself together. My injuries were not catastrophic, I was recovering. Just as well, because this was not over. I looked again at the guy with the knife. Blood was dripping from the blade. Then it dawned on me who he was: Crazy Bobby! Bobby Traveller. He glanced over at me, as a smirk formed on his ugly face. He knew I had recognised him.

Kenny noticed this, and laughed, "Surprised to see Bobby, are you, Hugo?"

Bobby and the other thug joined in with the laughter, then suddenly Kenny pulled out a gun, and without hesitation shot the other thug in his abdomen. The gun shot sounded incredibly loud in the empty space, bouncing between the concrete floor, ceiling and walls before it quietened. The thug took a couple of unsteady steps backwards, clutching his abdomen, with a look of utter confusion and disbelief on his face. A startled question started to form on his lips, but was cut short as he suddenly fell backwards – lifeless. I looked at Kenny and then quickly over at Bobby, who was standing with the knife still in his hand, his face hard and closed. They were exchanging glances and nods, so I knew something bad was about to happen to me. Bobby quickly turned, took a step towards Angus and stabbed him twice, in the chest and stomach. Angus cried out in pain, before his head dropped forward, the life ebbing away from him. I watched in revulsion, too weak to move. I knew I was next, and that I couldn't do anything to prevent it.

Bobby stepped back and roughly cut through the rope that had been holding Angus' right arm down, then Kenny placed the weapon in Angus' right hand, aimed it at the dead thug and fired another shot. Kenny then turned the gun towards me and fired the third shot, which hit me on the left side of my abdomen. A burning pain exploded from the entry wound, initially overwhelming me.: the pain was severe, beyond anything I'd ever experienced. I'd never actually been shot before, and the impact knocked the wind right out of me, but I managed to remain sitting up, and to keep my eyes on Kenny. He was walking towards me, triumph dancing in his evil eyes. I cursed the man. He had swapped places with Bobby, who was now holding the gun for the dying Angus.

"Impressed, Hugo? I haven't had much time to plan this scenario – had to improvise here. Your damned brother and Julia, almost derailed my plan – almost, but not quite! I think it still might fly. You and Grant ...," Kenny paused and looked over at the dead thug lying behind him. His insanity was vividly evident in his eyes as he returned his focus to me, saying, "So, this is how it goes: you and Grant attack Angus, desperate to find the pot of missing money, but you haven't done your homework properly, and Angus fights back, killing you both before he buys the ticket himself ... All right, it's a bit thin, but do you think the coppers will care? Angus' fingerprints on the gun, gun powder residue on him, Grant's fingerprints on the knife, and you all dead: case closed! What do you think?"

I didn't reply, I wasn't going to give him the benefit of my opinion of his sordid plot. He squatted awkwardly in front of me, smirking with self-satisfaction.

"If I thought you knew where the money was, then I'd make you talk, but luckily for you, Hugo, I know you don't! You haven't heard the latest, have you?" Kenny paused for dramatic effect, he just couldn't help himself.

"Your brother's escaped, yep, on his way to the High Court this morning. Drama in the street, Edinburgh's never seen anything like it: two cars stopped the prison van and blew the doors off. Douglas Storm, what a guy, I can't help but like him! Could do with a guy like that on my crew ... shame I gotta track him down and kill him – that's after I've taken care of Petite, and then your wives and kids ... exterminate the Storms. Sounds like a plan to me."

Kenny stopped his rant and waited. I didn't reply, just sat defiantly staring him in the eye. I wasn't going to plead for my life, I wasn't going to give him that satisfaction.

"You got guts, Hugo, I'll give you that ... Bobby let's end this!"

Kenny stood up, then another gun shot rang out. I closed my eyes, steeling myself for the inevitable, but I didn't feel any impact! Daring to peek, I saw Kenny swaying, his eyes bulging wide in shock, then he collapsed right in front of me. Bobby was getting up from behind a dead Angus, cursing as he aimed the gun. But he was too late – he'd made the mistake of leaving his cover, proving that he was just a street thug, used to brawling, and not a gun slinger skilled in shoot-outs. Another two shots were fired in quick succession, the second hitting Bobby right in the face, throwing him backwards. I tried to turn towards where the gun fire had come from, but the struggle made me pass out.

I came to as my head hit the floor. I didn't feel any pain, just felt cold, so very cold. The bitter, salty taste of blood was in my mouth. I spat and tried very hard to focus on the shadowy shape of a man moving fast towards me. He dropped to his knees and ripped open my shirt, quickly inspecting my wound. Then he applied pressure to the entry point with some sort of dressing. It seemed like a futile gesture; I could sense the life ebbing away from me. I looked at his serious face, and slowly began to recognise who it was.

"Douglas, what ...," I began but my voice failed me.

Douglas gently laid a finger on my lips. His chiselled face, pale after several months locked in a prison cell, softened as he gamely tried to smile. "Hush, don't speak, Hugo, just listen: you will be okay. I've called the ambulance, they shouldn't be too long ..."

Douglas fought back his tears. I looked at my big brother and felt the love between us. The man was a criminal and had done things most civilised people would characterise as evil, but I didn't care; he was my brother, my only kin, and the one who had saved my sorry skin yet again. I grabbed his hand and pulled myself up. I wasn't in pain, just felt numb. And this tiredness was overwhelming me, I just wanted to sleep ... close my eyes and let go – but I knew couldn't, not yet anyway.

"Don't you start crying on me here, Doug – that will kill me," I whispered, and paused to find some energy to continue. Doug smiled and was about to say something, but I spoke first. "Now tell me, Doug, you involved in this?" Douglas hesitated, but I squeezed his hand and whispered, "Don't lie to me."

"Yes ... yes, I was never going to rot in a cell, Hugo, you know that. And do you know how much money it takes to escape and disappear nowadays? A lot! Millions – and I didn't have millions, and neither did Julia. She's coming with me, we're disappearing together. Sorry about what happened to you; I didn't think Angus would involve you ... I should've though ... sorry." Douglas paused, and I squeezed his wrist again – I needed more. If I survived this, I'd have to pay – that was fine – but I wanted to learn more. I felt I'd earned that.

"Okay, Hugo, we knew Kenny was coming back, and that was bad news for Julia. She'd heard from Spain that Kenny was partially blaming her for what'd happened to him. His drug organisation was falling apart, and he was coming back quicker than we thought. We needed millions in cash – and quick. The poker game was my idea, and I was stupid enough to involve Angus. But only he could get in touch with me to get the key to my last cash reserve."

Douglas rolled up his sleeve, showing me a scar and I saw that he had a small key surgically implanted in his arm. Douglas looked around as he heard something, but I was too far gone to pick out what it was. I kept my eyes on my brother.

"Douglas, you coming? We don't have long," shouted a familiar female voice from the door.

"Julia?" I murmured. Douglas nodded, and was about to shout something back to her when I tightened my grip with my last ounce of energy, and whispered, "Listen, Doug – and this is final: you go now, and don't get caught! Disappear ... far away."

My vision started to fade. A blurry Douglas looked back at me and a tear rolled down his cheek and plopped onto my forehead. Then he kissed my forehead, gently laid my head down and got up.

I vaguely heard him running away as the darkness cradled me ever closer and I experienced a sense of floating towards a void of some kind. Behind me I thought I saw my children standing close together in the distance, holding each other tightly, all gathered around Emily. She was being brave for them, herself, and me. I felt my heart splinter into a million fragments as she waved: she could see me! I tried desperately to wave back, but my arms were useless; I could only watch. It felt like I was being propelled forwards towards some kind of a tunnel, and within this tunnel I thought I could see what looked like an owl: a symbol of wisdom. But was it really there, or was it merely in my mind's eye? I couldn't tell, but it looked real, and was strikingly black against the white emptiness beyond.

I concentrated on the owl's eyes, looming larger and larger as I seemed to be getting closer to the tunnel, and I wondered what this could all mean ...

Its cold, wide-open eyes seemed to be studying me intensely as I approached, reminding me of something Father Angus had said to me at the start of this escapade – and then it finally dawned on me, and I understood: whether in reality or in my own subconscious, I was being judged ...

About the Author

Anton Lindbak was born in Norway. He has lived in Scotland since 2001, finding the wet, cold and dark days much like home. He has more than a decade's experience working in hospital Emergency departments, and has seen it all. However, more than anything else, he loves to write, crime fiction and thrillers most of all. He is busy writing more Hugo Storm Crime Thrillers.

Printed in Great Britain
by Amazon